Illustrated
WELSH
FOLK TALES
FOR YOUNG
AND OLD

Peter Stevenson

The History Press

First published 2023

The History Press
97 St George's Place, Cheltenham,
Gloucestershire, GL50 3QB
www.thehistorypress.co.uk

British Library Cataloguing in Publication Data.
A catalogue record for this book is available from the British Library.

ISBN 978 1 80399 097 2

Typesetting and origination by The History Press.
Printed and bound in Turkey by Imak.

*To Valériane Leblond,
for all the breakfasts
at Medina*

Storytelling

Storyteller is *storïwr* in Welsh. The old word is *cyfarwydd*. And the stories in this book are the folk tales I love to tell. It's a sneaky peek into a storyteller's repertoire in the 2020s. You'll meet the rowdy mermaids of Cardigan Bay, the hidden lands below the sea, an ancient tree with a door into the otherworld, an old woman who makes love potions and mischief, the wise old toad who lives in a bog and knows everything, a clever girl who transforms into a swan, a green man who lives in no one's land, the enchantress who swallows a poet, a herd of fairy cattle who live beneath a lake, a boy who wears a frock to stop a castle being built, and an elephant who may or may not have died in Tregaron.

Many of these stories are old. Much older than me or your granny. Some are ancient. They were told by storytellers long ago, mostly in Welsh, some in Welsh Romany, others in English, and maybe in Polish, Somali, Swahili, Māori and Norwegian, for people have migrated to Wales from all over the world and brought their stories with them.

Folk tales are memories of real events mixed with dreams, then transformed by the imaginations of storytellers in a moment of telling. Siani Chickens, the woman in the illustration on the previous page, lived on the beach at Cei Bach over 100 years ago (see page 47). Beti Grwca is a character from a story, who may or may not have once been real (see page 51). That's why asking, 'Are folk tales true?' is not the right question.

The stories of Siani and Beti were told by Myra Evans, who heard them from her family and the old sea captains of Cei Newydd. Myra filled sketchbooks with drawings of the characters in the stories and the people who told them. She was a visual storyteller.

I began painting the illustrations in this book on Ynys Enlli, Bardsey Island, in May 2022, though I had already sketched many of the characters. The two sketches of Siani and Beti on this page were painted long before I first told their stories, because I like to describe pictures rather than remember words. This is visual storytelling.

And sometimes I show the sketches while I'm telling the stories, as if the pictures have leapt off the page of a book. I also make crankies – long, painted scrolls that move inside a big wooden box when you turn a handle, like a storyboard for an animated film.

Turn to page 171 to make your own mini-crankie.

To tell one of these stories, first read it out loud. Then close your eyes and try to repeat it. There's no need to memorise it unless you want to. Think of a story as a fence where the posts are the main events in the narrative that never change. The rest of the words are like the chicken wire in between that wobbles in the wind. Then all you need is a friend to tell your story to.

You may be holding a book in your hands, but these stories only come alive for a moment when a *storïwr* tells them. They are about transformation in ourselves and our weird world, our friendships and hopes, fears of rising sea levels and scary sounds at night. Just ask those Welsh mountains. They have lived longer than we have. They have listened to birdsong and the sound of rivers and sea. They have heard these tales before.

The Land beneath the Sea

Next time you're sitting on the beach looking across Cardigan Bay and trying to stop the gulls eating your chips, think about this. All that sea between Wales and Ireland was once rivers, lakes, forests and swamps where herds of deer and mammoth roamed. When the weather warmed, the ice in the mountains melted, the valleys flooded and dolphins and mermaids moved in.

The land was Maes Gwyddno, named after a mighty warrior, Gwyddno Garanhir. Though perhaps it should have been called Mererid, after his clever daughter who kept the floodwater at bay by opening and closing the sluice gates to control the amount of seawater flowing onto the land. She was the lady of the sea defences.

One evening, Mererid was gazing at the night sky and wondering whether the stars were exploding planets or the eyes of gods, while her father and another mighty warrior, Seithenyn, were partying in celebration of their latest victory in battle over their many enemies.

Seithenyn invited Mererid to join the party.

'No thanks, I prefer dolphins to hairy men with swords.'

A storm gathered out to sea. Mererid hurried to close
the sluice gates, but the sea rushed in and Gwyddno's
land was taken by a great flood, just as he had taken
it in battle. In time, the land beneath the sea
became a memory of rising sea levels
and melting ice and was named
Cantre'r Gwaelod.

There was another fabled land in Cardigan Bay, where the people cared for the forests, rivers and animals, and if they felled a tree or caught a fish, they always left an offering of food in exchange.

This was the land of Plant Rhys Ddwfn, the Children of Rhys the Deep. Not deep as in below the water. Rhys was a thinker, a philosopher, and he planted a hedge of herbs to hide his land from our ancestors' eyes. Only if someone stood on the one patch of herbs that grew on the coast would they see Rhys's world, but no one knew where that patch of herbs was, so all they ever saw was rain.

Rhys's children had children of their own and their children had children too. Their numbers grew, they felled more trees to build wooden homes and soon there wasn't enough land to grow food, so they cleared more forests. They made quilts and iron cauldrons, and built boats so they could visit the market in Aberteifi to sell their crafts and raise money to buy corn to make flour to bake bread. They traded with a man called Gruffydd ap Einion, a kind man who dreamed of a better world, and whose corn was fresh and prices fair.

One day, Rhys's children took Gruffydd to the patch of herbs on the coast, where he saw a land rich beyond his dreams, with all the wisdom of the world kept safely in forests and books. In his excitement, he stepped away from the herbs and never saw Rhys's land again, though he never forgot his dreams of a better world, and traded with his friends all his life.

Rhys's dreamworld is still there, hidden behind the mist and the stories of Gwyddno's land and Mererid's sea defences. And if you look hard enough, you might see it. Next time you're on the little train on the Cambrian Line as it trundles along the coast, look through the window, beyond your reflection and out to sea, and you may see Rhys's beautiful land in your mind, like Gruffydd did many years ago. For the sea keeps no secrets.

Oh, and Plant Rhys Ddwfn, in west Wales, is a colloquial name for those who lived here before.

The hidden people.

Y tylwyth teg.

The fairies.

Mermaids

Môrferch and her sisters have lived in Cardigan Bay ever since the mammoths left. They've been spotted near Aberteifi, Abergwaun, Aberystwyth, Aberbach and lots from Llanina alone. Yet most people don't think they've seen one, perhaps because the environmental services mistake them for dolphins and seals – and recently, a walrus.

Back in the Old Welsh Dreamtime, three brothers lived in a yellow, lime-washed farmhouse at the end of the Old Welsh Tramping Road on the shores of Cardigan Bay. Eldest Brother farmed the land and had honey on his bread, Middle Brother sailed the sea and had sugar in his porridge, while Little Brother wandered the Tramping Road playing tunes on his fiddle in exchange for beans on toast.

The two elder brothers were tired of doing all the work while Little Brother dreamed the days away, so they gave him a small, enchanted pig and told him to sell it to raise money to buy salt and beer. 'And don't swap it for magic beans or anything that makes wishes come true. Remember what happened last time.'

So Little Brother set off along the Old Welsh Tramping Road with a tune on his lips, fiddle on his back and an enchanted pig on a rope. He walked until he came to a deep, dark wood and a crooked house with a red door, and there stood a woman with a thousand wrinkles round her eyes.

'Would you like to buy an enchanted pig?' asked Little Brother.

The woman pulled on the one grey hair in the middle of her chin, 'Mmm! I'd like a little roast pork! I'll swap my enchanted handmill for your pig. It will make your wildest wishes come true.'

The pig hid behind Little Brother's legs.

Little Brother remembered what Eldest Brother had said: 'Don't swap it for anything that makes wishes come true,' but he couldn't resist a magic handmill, and the last thing he heard as the red door closed behind him was the squealing of a pig.

Oh, don't worry.

This is a fairy tale.

You can be the storyteller – maybe the pig ran up the chimney, slid down the roof, built a house of bricks, chased off a big, bad wolf and lived happily ever after?

Little Brother walked back along the Old Welsh Tramping Road, tune on his lips, fiddle on his back and an enchanted handmill under his arm. As he came to the shores of Cardigan Bay, he decided he'd like a home of his own.

'Little mill, little mill, grind me a handsome house,

Little mill, little mill, grind it without a mouse.'

The handmill began to grind and, in the blink of an eye, there stood a pink-washed longhouse filled with honey, beans and porridge.

Eldest Brother knocked on the door, 'Little Brother, where did this house come from? Last time I saw you, you were as poor as a church mouse. Did you sell the pig?'

'Sort of. I swapped it for an enchanted handmill.'

Eldest Brother took the handmill to his lime-washed farmhouse, placed it on the table, and made a wish.

'Little mill, little mill, grind me beer and women.

Oh, and a little fish for my tea.' (Eldest Brother was a rubbish poet.)

The handmill began to grind, and the kitchen filled with beer and women with fish tails, the door burst open and a river of beer poured down into Cardigan Bay, where Eldest Brother drowned with a mermaid on either arm.

At that moment, Middle Brother returned to Cardigan Bay in his red-masted ship laden with a cargo of salt, and he found himself surrounded by mermaids singing rowdy sea shanties, inviting his crew to remove their trousers and leap into the beery water. Most of them did, but Middle Brother anchored the ship, went ashore and knocked on the door of the pink-washed longhouse.

'Little Brother, when I last saw you, you were as poor as a cabin boy. And where have all these mermaids come from?'

Little brother told him about the handmill, which was still grinding out beer and mermaids. Middle Brother took the handmill to his ship.

'Little mill, little mill, grind me salty salt.

Little mill, little mill, grind it without a fault.'

The handmill began to grind and the deck filled with salt, until the ship creaked under the weight, broke in two and sank to the bottom of the beery, salty sea, where Middle Brother, too, drowned with a mermaid on either arm.

And the handmill is still grinding on the deck of the sunken ship, and that's why swimming in Cardigan Bay is like frolicking with beery, salty mermaids.

Afanc

When Wales was wilder than it is now, a monstrous Afanc crawled out of a pool on the Conwy River, tore down trees, built dams, destroyed crops and flooded the land. It was a wild and hairy creature with a scaly tail and huge yellow teeth, and the people wanted rid of it. They needed a Hero.

Enter Huw Gadarn, Huw the Mighty, who arrived in Conwy riding his plough pulled by two long-horned oxen, the Ychen Bannog, the children of the Spotted Cow. Huw could tame wild and hairy creatures. He had turned wild boar into pigs, red jungle fowl into chickens and longhorn cattle into Welsh Blacks. He was the first Welsh Farmer. And he wore wellies.

Huw spoke, '*Ffrindiau*! Friends! I need a volunteer to be the bait to trap the Afanc.'

The people pulled their hoods over their heads and mumbled something about it being past their bedtime or having to wash their hair.

'You!' said Huw, pointing at a girl who sat quietly reading a book beneath a crack willow that overhung the river.

'Why do I have to be bait?' she asked.

'The Afanc will be attracted to you,' said Huw the Mighty, 'Then I will leap out, slay the wild and hairy monster, and save the day. It's what I do.'

'The Afanc isn't a monster. Leave it alone. It's cute,' and the girl went back to her book while Huw kept watch.

At twilight, the pool began bubbling and out crawled the Afanc, dripping with pondweed, thrashing its scaly tail and gnashing its yellow teeth. It stared into the girl's eyes, she held out her arm, it sniffed her hand, she stroked its fur and it laid its head on the book in her lap.

'Don't worry,' she said, 'No one's going to hurt you.'

In that moment of tenderness, mighty Huw leapt out from behind a tree and posed like a teapot.

Huw chained the Afanc, tied it to his plough and ordered the Ychen Bannog to drag it away. The Afanc whimpered and tried to hold on to the girl, but the horned cattle hauled it down the Conwy Valley and through Bwlch Rhiw'r Ychen, the Pass of the Oxen. The strain was so great on one of the oxen that its eyeball popped out at Llyn-y-Foel, which became Pwll Llygad Ych, Pool of the Ox's Eye.

At Llyn Glaslyn, Huw looked into the Afanc's watery eyes. The girl was right. It wasn't monstrous. It was cute. So, he released it into the lake and resolved not to tell anyone that he hadn't slain it.

Huw the Mighty was greeted in Conwy as a Hero, while the girl sat quietly beneath the willow tree reading her book, *The Natural History of Beavers*.

In Welsh, *Afanc* means Beaver. They used to build dams in the shape of willow bowers at Cilgerran on the Teifi, until they became extinct eight hundred years ago. Now, they're being reintroduced and the Afanc will swim in Welsh rivers once more, thanks to people like the clever girl of Conwy.

The Fairy Cow

It was Calan Mai, the first day of summer. Green Girl stood up to her waist in Llyn Barfog, the Bearded Lake, dripping with pondweed, twisting her red hair into plaits and decorating them with ivy and holly, while her herd of milk-white fairy cattle grazed on the meadowsweet that grew round the banks. She watched as a young farmer ran down the hill from Cwm Dyffryn Gwyn like an eager puppy. He was a poet, a *bardd gwlad*, so it was no surprise when he fumbled in his pocket and gave her a stale cheese sandwich. She laughed like a donkey, called her cattle and vanished into the water.

This went on for days, months, years. She didn't know how long because time passed slowly in her world beneath the water where there were no clocks, no time, no night or day. A moment down there was a lifetime above.

When Calan Mai came round again, Green Girl stood up to her waist in the lake as if time had stood still. One of her fairy cows followed the scent of fresh hay to Cwm Dyffryn Gwyn, where the old farmer led her to the cowshed thinking she was a wild cow. He fed her on the finest hay and she gave him the foamiest, frothiest milk, cream and cheese. She fell in love with one of his Welsh Blacks and soon she was mother to a herd of sturdy cattle. The farmer became rich beyond his dreams.

Time passed quickly above the water and, in the blink of an eye, the fairy cow grew old. Instead of putting her out to pasture to thank her for all she had given, the farmer called the butcher, who raised his knife. Green Girl's shriek pierced the air and the butcher's arm froze above his head. The fairy cow mooed and ran to Llyn Barfog, and where she dived into the water, a white waterlily flowered.

The children of the fairy cow, Welsh Blacks and Milk-Whites, followed their mother and Green Girl counted them into the lake in the old way, '*Un dau tri pedwar pump*', move a stone from one hand to the other, '*Un dau tri pedwar pump*', another stone, until the lake turned white with waterlilies.

The old farmer ran down the hill from Cwm Dyffryn Gwyn and stared at Green Girl, just as he did when he was a young poet many years before. His face was weathered and his hands wrinkled, while she didn't look a day older than when they first met. His hand shook as he gave her a stale cheese sandwich. She laughed like a donkey and vanished beneath the water.

Every summer, Llyn Barfog turns to snow when the waterlilies blossom, a memory of the story of the fairy cow.

It's weird to think that you could be told to leave your home because your valley was about to be drowned to build a giant reservoir to supply drinking water to a big city. But that's what happened in the 1960s to the children who lived around Capel Celyn in Cwm Tryweryn, where they swam in the river, ran to school each morning, sat at wooden desks, dipped pens in inkwells, sang songs and wrote stories in lined exercise books. Teacher Mrs Roberts read their names in the register: Ann Elizabeth Jones, Arfon Jones, Elwyn Rowlands, Eurgain Jones, Euron Jones, Geraint Jones, Jane Watkin Jones, Lowri Mair Jones, Rhian Jones and Tryweryn Evans.

Shortly after the school closed, the children and their families left their homes for the last time. Welsh dressers and beds were loaded into vans and taken to new houses above the valley, cattle and sheep were moved from the farms, elm trees were felled, onions and *tatws* were dug up from vegetable patches, net curtains flapped in the breeze and the gravestones of ancestors were moved to a new chapel.

Bulldozers flattened the old school building and the waters of Llyn Celyn flooded the village. The children started next term in new schools at Cwm Tirmynach and Maesywaen.

During a heatwave in 2022, there was so little water in Llyn Celyn that the ghostly submerged houses reappeared, along with memories of Hafod Fadog, Bryn Ifan, Y Ganedd Lyd, Cae Fado, Y Gelli, Pen Y Bryn Mawr, Ty'n Rhos, Gwerndelw, Tyncerrig, Maesydail. And the drowning gave Wales a new creation myth to sit alongside the forgotten fairy tales of dreamers who built utopian lands out at sea, old ladies who made love potions with well water and rivers who were seen as people.

The graffiti on the wall of Troed-y-Rhiw, a ruined cottage near Llanrhystud, says '**Cofiwch Dryweryn**'. Remember Tryweryn. It occasionally gets painted over, but by the morning, the words are back. Water never keeps secrets.

The Red Lady

Siôn the Painter was a dreamer, a tall, happy lad who painted houses and canvases, while at night he played his fiddle at dances around Aberaeron in exchange for a meal. He was such a good fiddler that blackbirds and thrushes sang along to his tunes, although as a dancer, he fell over his own feet.

One evening after painting the vicarage in Nantcwnlle, Siôn was walking home over Trychrug Hill when darkness fell and he couldn't see the path in front of his nose. A ghost owl flew over his head, a fox stared with yellow eyes before loping away, and he realised he might fall into a swamp and never be seen again, like many fiddlers before him.

Then he saw a light. He thought it was Tŷ-clottas, old Pegi's house, but as he approached, it moved in a circle. Every bone in his body told him to run, for this was the tylwyth teg, and they cast spells on silly lads like him. As he turned, a girl in a scarlet dress dragged him into a ring of dancers.

Siôn danced with the girl in scarlet and his gangly legs and arms flew in all directions, though he didn't fall over his own feet, not once. Glow worms lit the dark, a smell of honeysuckle filled the air and there stood an elegant lady dressed in a flowing, red gown.

'Who are you, Mortal?' asked the Red Lady.

'I'm Siôn. I'm a painter. Walls and pictures,' he replied with a grin.

The Red Lady laughed. 'We have no need of painters. We are art. We are nature. We do not grow old. Do you have anything else to offer us, Mortal?'

Siôn took out his fiddle and played, but no one danced.

'Didn't you like my playing, ma'am?'

'We are Welsh fairies. That is not our tune,' said the Red Lady, so Siôn launched into 'Dawns Eldorai', learned from a Welsh Romany friend, and the dancers whirled all night long.

'Mortal Man,' said the Red Lady, 'You have pleased us. You have a wish.'

Siôn wished he could play every year for the dancers of Trychrug, and he held the hand of the girl in scarlet and puckered his lips for a kiss, when he heard a voice. He opened his eyes and found himself sat in a ditch, being licked on the cheek by Pegi Tŷ-clottas's mangy sheepdog.

'Is that you, Siôn the Dreamer?' shouted Pegi. 'I heard music and saw the light, and thought it was a corpse candle come to take me away, but it's only silly Siôn with soggy feet playing his fiddle.'

Siôn grumbled, 'I was about to kiss a fairy!'

Pegi took his hand, 'Poor Siôni. Let's get you home and clean you up.'

From that day, Siôn told the story of how he became fiddler to the Red Lady and would have married a fairy but for Pegi's mangy old sheepdog.

Most people just smiled, 'Poor Siôni. Always dreaming.'

Though they wondered where he'd learned those wicked dance moves.

The Little Red Man

In Cwm Gido, the Valley of the Goats, lived a boy called Guto, who had a big, wide smile and a kind, warm heart, and at the end of one leg he had a great big club foot. He dragged it behind him when he walked, and the children laughed and called him 'Big Foot', but little Mari from Penrhiw loved to creep up behind him and kiss him when he wasn't looking.

One day, Guto sat by the stream at Tyddyn-y-Cwm listening to the rattling water and the song of the wagtails, because the birds and the stream didn't laugh at him. He heard shouting and turned around to see something struggling to escape from a bramble bush. Guto thought it was a hare, so he pulled the brambles away and found himself face to face not with a hare, but a little red man.

When he saw Guto, the little man stopped wriggling and froze. Guto carefully lifted him free of the brambles, stood him on the ground and told him to be more careful next time or he might fall into a nettle patch.

The little man wobbled on long legs and pointed at Guto, 'You have a wish.'

Guto wished for two legs the same length and two feet the same size.

'Done,' said the little man, and he plucked a leaf from an oak tree, rolled it into a cone, filled it with water from the well at Pistyll y Rhiw, and told Guto to drink three times. Then he vanished, as little red men do in fairy tales round here.

Guto drank and fell into a sleep. When he awoke, he remembered his wish and stood up. His legs were exactly the same length. He did a little dance of happiness, then fell flat on his face. For now he had **TWO** great big club feet.

Well, Guto's wish had come true, he had two feet the same size, and he was happy enough. He could run without limping, the boys didn't laugh and Mari from Penrhiw could only catch him if he wanted a kiss.

As time passed, Guto and Mari fell in love, and lived at the little cottage in the valley of the goats, which became known as Lover's Lane.

The House with the front door at the back

An old farmer with a stubbly chin lived in a damp house at Deunant, near Aberdaron. Every morning, he padded down the creaky stairs in his socks, stepped outside the front door, dropped his trousers, and …

'Eeeuw!' Yes, I know, but the poor man didn't have a bathroom or a *tŷ bach*, and his muck heap was great for growing potatoes.

One evening, he sat there, trousers round his ankles, when he became aware he was being watched by two little people covered from head to toe in poo.

The little woman spoke, 'We have lived here long before you were born and we have never meant any harm. Yet every evening, we sit by our fireside with our baby, and you poo down our chimney.'

The little man added, 'If you don't believe us, step on my foot three times.'

The old farmer stepped on the little man's foot and there, next to his front doorstep, was a tiny, red-roofed house splattered with poo.

Stretching out in front of his eyes was a village of houses and cobblestone streets. People dressed in strange fashions, waistcoats, tall hats and aprons, walked around as if he wasn't there. Herds of white cattle and enchanted pigs fed on scraps in every alleyway. The farmer knew he had passed through the veil into the otherworld of the tylwyth teg. He blinked, and the town vanished.

The old farmer had never meant to harm the hidden people, so he caught the bus to Pwllheli to buy a bathroom from Bonmarché, but they were expensive and he had a hedgehog in his pocket. So, he unscrewed his front door, piled stones in the doorway and painted it with lime mortar, so he would never again poop on the little family. And he planted his muck heap with evening primroses and night-scented stocks till the air smelled so sweet. Then he knocked a doorway in his back wall, made a new muck heap by the doorstep, and hoped there were no little people living there.

And that is the story of the house in Aberdaron with the front door at the back.

Siani Chickens

*A*mser maith yn ôl / A long time ago.

On the little beach at Cei Bach stood *pump /* five ramshackle cottages.

One fell down, and then there were *pedwar* / four.

Then *tri* / three.

Dau / two.

Until there was only *un* / one ramshackle cottage left.

Smoke poured through the thin thatch on the roof, the windows were stuffed with rags and in the doorway sat a woman with clogs on her feet and a red-and-yellow-spotted handkerchief round her head. There were chickens everywhere.

This was Siani Pob Man.

Siani earned a penny or two telling fortunes to the visitors who flocked to Cei Newydd for their holidays, and if anyone dared to suggest she couldn't see the future, she chased them away, but not until she had sold them a picture postcard of herself cuddling one of her chickens.

They all had names. Bidi, Ledi, Ruth, Charlotte, Marged, Lisa, Beti, Kit, Cynddylan and Jonathan, the cockerel. They lived in Siani's cottage, and laid eggs in every corner.

Siani sold the eggs from door to door. Everyone bought them because they loved Siani, but no one ate them as they tasted of salt and seaweed. So, she dyed them in strong tea to make them a more attractive brown colour, but still no one ate them as they still tasted of salt and seaweed.

Siani loved children as much as her chickens. When a grumpy shopkeeper in Llanarth was rude to the children, she told him he should be ashamed of himself. He was a nasty, old, stubble-chinned man who should be kind to those who weren't as wealthy as he was.

Siani told stories, and her favourite was how her heart was broken by love so she went to live with the Welsh Romany. Then she looked after her mam in Aberaeron, before she moved to the ramshackle cottage at Cei Bach, in the no-man's-land between the cliffs and sea, where she paid rent to no man. There were no boundaries to Siani's world.

People asked if she was lonely, but Siani said, 'No! I have my chickens, the children come to play, the miners from Rhymney listen to my stories and Mr Morgan visits twice a day!'

Mr Morgan often stormed in through Siani's front door and flooded her home. So, she climbed the ladder into the crog-loft and stayed with her chickens in her four-poster bed, which was sawn off to fit under the rafters, and there she waited till Mr Morgan left. Mr Morgan. *Y Môr.* The Sea. Her dearest friend.

Siani was born at Fferm Bannau Duon, in Llanarth, and her real name was Jane Leonard. Everyone thought she was poor, but she kept a biscuit tin under her bed that contained £120 in threepenny bits, which she gave to the orphans and sick children of Aberaeron.

Although her cottage is long gone, children still play on the beach at Cei Bach and Mr Morgan always visits twice a day, looking for his true love.

Beti's Love Potions

In a mud-walled cottage on the slopes of Banc Penrhiw, near Cei Newydd, lived a mischievous old woman named Beti Grwca. She had a thousand wrinkles round her eyes, a single grey hair in the middle of her chin and a solitary yellow tooth that wobbled unnervingly in the breeze from her breath. Beti made potions with herbs from the forest mixed with water from the well at Pistyll y Rhiw, but not any old potions. Beti made love potions.

One day, the childminder from Plas-y-Wern called to see Beti for a drop of potion, and with her was the squire's baby boy, Cedrig. At the same time, the farm-girl from Rhyd-y-Ferwig arrived for her dose, with the farmer's baby daughter, Elinor. Beti gave the two girls their potions, but being a mischievous

old granny, she also gave a drop to the two babies and cackled to herself, as troublesome old ladies do in fairy tales.

Time passed in the blink of a crow's eye, and Beti Grwca was still there at Banc Penrhiw, even more wrinkles around her eyes, more mischievous than ever and still selling love potions. One day, a girl knocked on the door, and while Beti

mixed a potion from the green and brown bottles on her sagging shelves, there was another knock and a lad asked for a drink of water.

As the eyes of the two young people met, they rushed into each other's arms and began kissing, right there in the middle of Beti's flagstone floor. Beti pushed them apart with a frying pan and asked their names. The girl said 'Elinor' and the lad, 'Cedrig'.

Beti explained that they were the babies she had given potions to, and now they were doomed to be in love for evermore.

Not that Elinor or Cedrig were bothered. They held hands in Aberystwyth, cuddled in Aberteifi and kissed in Aberaeron, and after a year they decided to get married. But Cedrig's father, the old squire of Plas-y-Wern, didn't want his son to marry a poor farm girl like Elinor, while Elinor's mother didn't want her daughter

to marry into a well posh family like Cedrig's. So, the young couple took a boat across Cardigan Bay and got married in Barmouth.

When they returned from their honeymoon, the old Squire was two metres under the ground, so Cedrig and Elinor inherited Plas-y-Wern and they filled the house with so much love and so many babies they couldn't count them all, never mind remember all their names.

And Beti? Well, she's still there at Banc Penrhiw, though the solitary yellow tooth and grey hair dropped out long ago. And she's still making love potions, and it's said she's responsible for all the happy marriages in west Wales. And most of the troublesome ones.

Sgilti the Fiddler

If you follow the road from Llanarth to Gilfachreda, you'll come to an oakwood called Allt-y-Cefn. Years ago, many trees were chopped down to build a road straight through the middle of the wood, though had the woodcutters known the old stories, maybe they would have left the trees alone. You see, it's never wise to disturb the homes of the hidden people – y tylwyth teg.

In a clearing at Allt-y-Cefn stood an ancient, gnarled oak called Coeden y Brenin, the King Tree, where the tylwyth teg danced and a door opened into the otherworld. On the other side of the clearing was a thatched cottage called Bwlch-y-Cefn, where Grasi lived. Grasi knew she shared her home with the tylwyth teg, so each night before she went to bed, she left bread and cheese and milk on her oak kitchen table. Every morning when she awoke, the food was gone, her floor was scrubbed clean and on the table was a shiny silver coin. Grasi had never seen the tylwyth teg and felt she never should.

One evening, she was drifting to sleep in the ropes of the tylwyth teg when she heard the sound of a solitary fiddle. She leapt out of bed, wrapped her red patchwork quilt around her shoulders and ran to the top of the stairs. There, dancing in a circle were the hidden people, whirling round to the sound of a solitary fiddler. The faster he played, the faster the dancers danced, and they shouted, 'Slower, Sgilti, slower,' but Sgilti the fiddler played faster and faster, and round and round the dancers danced in a swirl of red, until they fell in a heap, arms and legs waving in the air, all laughing.

Grasi giggled, very quietly, but they heard her, and in the blink of a crow's eye they were gone. She ran down the creaky stairs to the doorway, but all she saw was Sgilti the fiddler leaping from branch to branch through the oaks like a squirrel till he reached the King Tree, where he disappeared into the otherworld. When Grasi reached the tree, there was no door to be seen.

From that day, the tylwyth teg never visited Grasi again, and she had to do all her own cleaning till her back ached and her hands were red raw. But at night, lying alone in her bed in the ropes of the tylwyth teg, she often heard the sound of Sgilti's fiddle as he leapt through the branches of the King Tree.

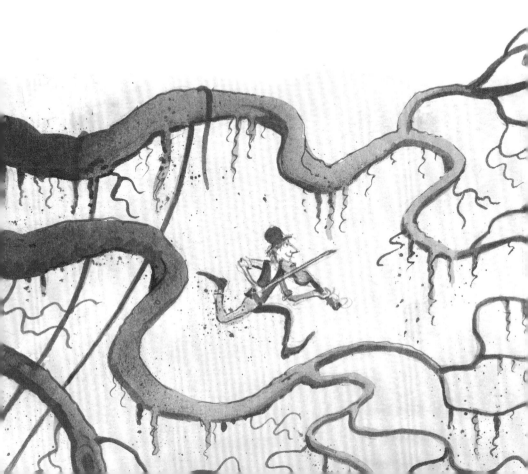

This all happened a long time ago, but the ruins of Grasi's cottage are still there, underneath a modern bungalow. A few years ago, a landslide closed the road through Allt-y-Cefn, yet still more trees are being felled, this time to build a caravan park. Maybe the woodcutters should listen to the old stories before the whole of Allt y Cefn is cut down and replaced with caravans. And then what would the visitors who stay in the caravans do, with no forest to enjoy on their holidays?

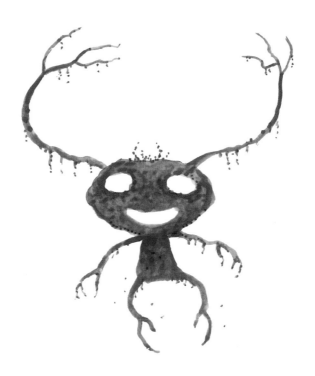

Shemi the Fibber

At 6 a.m. on 22 April 1912, Denys Corbett-Wilson took off in his Bleriot monoplane from a field overlooking the ferry terminal in Goodwick Harbour, and one hundred minutes later, he landed in a field at Enniscorthy, having completed the first flight from Wales to Ireland across the land of Plant Rhys Ddwfn. Five days later, Vivian Hewitt from Bodfari flew from Holyhead to Dublin, the first Welshman to make the journey, ten minutes faster than Corbett-Wilson, so starting an argument about who flew across the Irish Sea first. The answer was neither. It was an old fisherman and fibber from Goodwick.

Shemi Wâd lived in a white-washed cottage and worked as a fisherman, market gardener, farmhand, clock mender and pig sticker. Shemi told tall tales, spat into buckets, scratched himself in public and didn't believe in washing. That's why he had fleas. One was a singing flea, who lived under his bed in a saucepan he used as a chamber pot. The flea sang rude sea shanties, and no one sang better than Shemi's singing flea. It would have been a sensation on TikTok.

One sunny day, Shemi was fishing from his favourite rock at the Parrog. He felt in his pocket for some bait and pulled out some string, a box of matches, a piece of cheese, an unwashed hanky, a sweet covered in fluff and a stale currant bun. He threaded the bun on his fishing line, tied the rod to his tummy with the string, lit a fire with the matches, ate the cheese and the fluffy sweet, dabbed his mouth with the hanky and dreamed of fish for tea. The sharp-eyed gulls spotted the bun and started eating it, just as Shemi snored loudly and startled the birds, who took off, pulling the line behind them.

Shemi found himself flying over the sea, so he had an afternoon nap and when he awoke, he was high above a grey city. He asked the gulls to let him go, and he landed with a thump in a flower bed. He checked his hat was still on his head and asked a couple of passing ladies where he was, but they couldn't understand him. This was clearly Central Park, New York, where they didn't speak Pembrokeshire.

Shemi was tired after his long flight, so he climbed inside an old cannon that reminded him of the ones back home in Fishguard and went to sleep. In the morning, there was a loud bang and Shemi was flying over the sea again, but not attached to gulls. He landed with a thump on the grass at Pencw, checked his hat was still on his head, and told everyone in Goodwick about his day. No one believed him, of course. A flock of gulls could never have pulled Shemi over the sea to New York, now, could it? It was too far. They'd dropped him in Phoenix Park in Dublin. Again.

Last time it happened, he rode home on the back of a giant crab.

So there you are, Shemi Wâd was the first person to fly to Ireland.

And a great fibber.

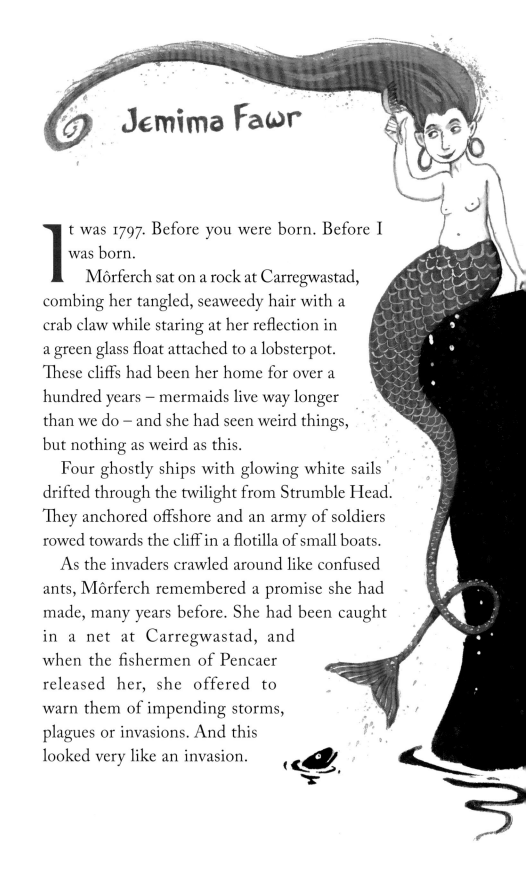

Jemima Fawr

I t was 1797. Before you were born. Before I
was born.

Môrferch sat on a rock at Carregwastad,
combing her tangled, seaweedy hair with a
crab claw while staring at her reflection in
a green glass float attached to a lobsterpot.
These cliffs had been her home for over a
hundred years – mermaids live way longer
than we do – and she had seen weird things,
but nothing as weird as this.

Four ghostly ships with glowing white sails
drifted through the twilight from Strumble Head.
They anchored offshore and an army of soldiers
rowed towards the cliff in a flotilla of small boats.

As the invaders crawled around like confused
ants, Môrferch remembered a promise she had
made, many years before. She had been caught
in a net at Carregwastad, and
when the fishermen of Pencaer
released her, she offered to
warn them of impending storms,
plagues or invasions. And this
looked very like an invasion.

So, she sang a song to call the fishermen and watched as her sisters dragged a boat down into the depths.

The fishermen of Pencaer heard the song and a soldier rode to the fort to prepare the Fishguard infantry for an invasion, while the wealthy folks at Tregwynt buried their treasure in the garden and barricaded the windows.

Môrferch watched her sisters sink another boat, then she wrapped herself in a blue shawl and followed a line of soldiers along the lane towards Llanwnda. They stopped at a farm where Colonel William S. Tate told Mr James that Trehowel was to be the headquarters of the Black Legion from revolutionary France while he negotiated the surrender of the Welsh troops.

This was a mess. Môrferch slid down the hill into town and through the shop door of Fishguard shoemaker Jemima Niclas, known as Jemima Fawr, because she was so strong. When she heard the news, Jemima rammed her black, floppy hat on her head, wrapped herself in a red shawl, picked up a pitchfork and called at every house until she raised an army of 400 women. She wrapped them in blue and red woollen shawls to look like soldiers, armed them with shovels and brushes, and they marched up the hill above the Parrog.

Jemima's soldiers marched round and round the hill to give the impression that the Welsh army was bigger than it actually was, but Colonel Tate wasn't fooled. He knew the old stories of women who dressed up as soldiers to scare away invading fleets of ships. What terrified him was that some of these ferocious Fishguard women had tails sticking out from beneath their skirts and several of his boats had already been sunk by the local mermaids. Tate knew he was beaten, so he ordered the Black Legion to surrender and Wales has never been invaded again, all thanks to Jemima. And Môrferch.

And the tail of the mermaid of Carregwastad is as true as when it was first told by the famous fibbers of Fishguard (see page 61).

The Boy who wore a frock

Siaci Ifan stood in front of the fireplace in his parents' stone cottage on Mynydd Bach, dressed in a skirt, an apron, a blouse, a shawl and a mop cap on his head. His father Dafydd smeared a little soot from last night's fire on his son's cheeks and nose to disguise him. Siaci didn't laugh. It was too serious. They were off to watch Mr Augustus Brackenbury's nice new house fall down.

Mr Brackenbury was an elegantly dressed gentleman from Lincolnshire, who had bought land on Mynydd Bach to build a castle, as many a visitor to Wales had done before. The people wondered how Augustus could buy land that didn't belong to anyone. The Mynydd was common land, shared by everyone, where they dug peat, quarried stone and kept goats and chickens. If anything, the land owned them.

Augustus Brackenbury built a house in Trefenter to live in while he designed his castle, and the roof timbers were in place, when he woke one morning to find it had fallen down. And there was Siaci Ifan, staring and looking fetching in his frock. Augustus asked Siaci if he had done this, but the boy said nothing. Augustus thought this was rude, but in fact, he was speaking a language the boy didn't understand. Siaci gave a twirl and stared some more.

Augustus built a second house, and that, too, fell down in the night. He built a third and kept watch till twilight when he saw a strange procession of people marching down the mountain towards him. They were all dressed in skirts and bonnets, some with beards, all armed with pickaxes and sledgehammers, and that night, Augustus's house fell to the ground.

To Augustus, this was war! And a few years later, he built his castle.

And it was a fine-looking castle, with turrets, towers and a moat.

One evening, when Augustus was away on business in Aberystwyth, Siaci blew his pibcorn, and they came, six hundred of them, maybe a thousand, from Llanilar, Lledrod and Llangwyryfon, all dressed in frocks. In a single night, Augustus's castle fell to the ground. In the morning, you wouldn't have known it had ever stood there. Even the moat was neatly filled in.

The event became known as *Rhyfel y Sais Bach*, and the war lasted for ten years. But who won? Not Augustus, because he left and never returned. Nor the people who lost their land and sailed on ships to the United States of America, where they took new land in Appalachia and Ohio. So I think Mynydd Bach itself won the war.

And Siaci? Well, he lived in Llangwyryfon, where he worked as a gravedigger in St Ursula's Church and always looked fetching in his frock.

The Old Toad

Back in the old Welsh Dreamtime, the birds decided to elect a King. They came from North and South, big birds and little, colourful and drab, twittering and squawking, and they agreed their King would be the bird who could fly the highest. Everyone knew Eagle would win, for he could soar high over Eryri.

But little Wren thought the birds needed a Queen.

So, she jumped onto Eagle's back and hid among his feathers. When Eagle flew higher than any other bird, Wren jumped from his back, flew just that little bit higher and sang loudly, 'I'm Queen now!'

5

Well, the birds twittered in anger. How could such a tiny, cheeky, loud-mouth be their Queen? They decided to drown her in a pan of their own tears, and it was almost full when clumsy old Owl, who couldn't see in daylight, tripped over her own feet, knocked over the pan and spilt everything.

So, Wren became Queen and made Eagle her King, and went off to live in the hedgerows, happy that a clever little bird with a loud voice could be heard above the angry twittering.

Eagle was a kindly King, but as time passed, he grew grumpy and gloomy. He had so many stories to tell but no one wanted to hear them. So, he decided to find a companion who would listen to his tales, but she would have to be as unimaginably old and boring as he was. It could only be

Owl, and not any old Owl. Owl of Cwmcawlwyd. But how old was she? It would be rude to ask her age, so he went to ask his friend, Stag of Rhedynfre. He found Stag dozing beneath a withered oak stump with branches that looked like his antlers.

'*Bore da*, Stag. How old is Owl?'

Stag snorted till the velvet fell from his antlers. 'See this oak tree? I remember it as an acorn. An oak is three hundred years growing, three hundred years in its prime, three hundred years withering and three hundred years dying. When it was an acorn, Owl was an ancient, wrinkled old bird. If you don't believe me, ask Salmon of Llyn Llaw.'

Eagle thanked Stag and found Salmon hiding beneath the bank of the lake.

'*P'nhawn dda*, Salmon. How old is Owl?'

Salmon poked her head out of the water, 'I am as old as the number of scales on my back and fins added together and multiplied by the spots on my belly. When I was a fry, Owl was an ancient, wrinkled old bird. If you don't believe me, ask Ousel of Cilgwri.'

So, Eagle thanked Salmon and found Ousel perched on a small stone on top of a mountain.

'*Noswaith dda*, Ousel. How old is Owl?'

'See this stone? It was once so big that the two mighty oxen, the Ychen Bannog, couldn't pull it. Every day, after dinner, I've wiped my beak on it until it became this tiny pebble. Imagine how long that has taken? Yet, when I was a fledgling, Owl was an ancient, wrinkled old bird. But if you don't believe me, ask the wise old Toad of Borth Bog.

Eagle thanked Ousel and flew west along the Dyfi River to Cors Fochno, where he found Toad sat among the sundews, looking for all the world like a leathery glove, blinking and breathing.

Eagle asked, 'Ah, Toad? I've decided Owl will be my companion, but I haven't asked her yet and she must be as unimaginably old and boring as I am. So, how old is Owl?'

More breathing and blinking, until Toad spoke, 'I am so old, I remember when all the earth was as high as the highest mountain.'

'I have eaten all the dust that once filled the valleys of Wales, from the tops of the mountains down to this bog. Yet I've only eaten one grain of dust a day, as it would not be sensible or sustainable to eat more. I am so old, I hardly remember being young, but when I was a tadpole, Owl was mindbogglingly, teethgrindingly, bumscratchingly wrinkled. She'll keep you awake all night with her endless twittering, but you won't mind, 'cos you're a dimwit.'

Eagle now knew that Owl was unimaginably old, so he thanked Toad and flew off to ask Owl to be his companion, as Toad croaked, 'Dimwit, Dimwit, Dimwit.'

You see, Toad is so wise he could solve every problem in the world, but no one has ever asked him because they drown in the bog before reaching him. Anyway, they wouldn't understand him, as people don't speak Toad.

That's why the world is in a mess.

Jac-y-do

Dan woke up one morning, rolled out of bed and ran barefoot down the creaky stairs in his jim-jams to find a little grey-black bird sat in the fireplace covered in soot. The jackdaw stared at him, squawked and flapped her wings, but she couldn't fly. She had fallen out of the nest in the chimney, bringing all the soot with her.

Dan opened the front door, 'Let's find your mam and dad, eh, Jaci?'

She followed him onto the terrace. He sat her in the branches of the Bardsey apple tree in the front yard so her parents could find her. As he fed her a worm from Mam's veg patch, next door's cat, Twts, watched and licked her paw with a red tongue and dreamed of bird cawl. Dan went to the kitchen to fetch a mop and bucket to clean the floor, and when he turned round, there was Jaci looking up at him.

Dan placed Jaci back in the tree
and went to the kitchen to make a cheese
sandwich for lunch. When he turned round,
there was Jaci. He shooed her outside and ran along
the terrace and down the road to school with Jaci following
behind. In the playground, another jackdaw peeped out of
Gwyn's backpack, while Sioned's sat on her shoulder like a
parrot. Ceri pushed hers around in a wheelbarrow, singing:

'Mi welais Jac-y-do
yn eistedd ar ben tô,
het wen ar ei ben a dwy goes bren
ho-ho-ho-ho-ho-ho.'

Through the summer holidays, Jaci followed Dan everywhere. She slept on his windowsill at night, waited outside the *tŷ bach*, and went for walks through the heather and gorse on the three mountains. He threw food into the air to teach her to fly and encourage her to return to the wild, but still she followed him.

Until one day he found her sitting on the roof, squawking with the other jackdaws. In the autumn she disappeared, though she returned in the winter to watch Dan dig a path through the snow to school. But when she tried to run after him, she slipped on the ice and froze her tail feathers.

In the spring, she built a nest in the chimney with a beak full of sticks. She fed worms to her own baby until it fell into the fireplace and sat there covered in soot. And all summer, Jaci's baby followed Dan around, just like its mam.

Twts watched all this and licked her paw with a red tongue, but Jac-y-do was far too clever for old puss-cat. She was free as a bird.

Swan Girl

A swan landed on the rocks on the coast of Gower, removed her white wings and feathers – and out stepped a girl. She smelled the air, swam in the sea and felt the salt water on her skin. All was well in her world, but … isn't there always a 'but' in fairy tales?

A young man was enchanted by her. He picked up her wings and feathers and held them to his cheek.

Swan Girl walked out of the water and told him to return her clothes.

He refused and said he loved her. She told him he knew nothing about her, she wasn't like him, she wasn't from his world and he was being silly.

She followed him to his cottage, where he locked her wings and feathers in an oak chest.

He gave her pretty dresses, but she longed for her cool feathers.

He lit the fire to dry her, but it wrinkled her skin.

He fed her rich food, but it gave her belly ache.

She lived in the bath filled with salt water.

At night he unlocked the chest and held her wings and feathers to his cheek.

And every night she watched as her sisters flew past the moon, free as birds.

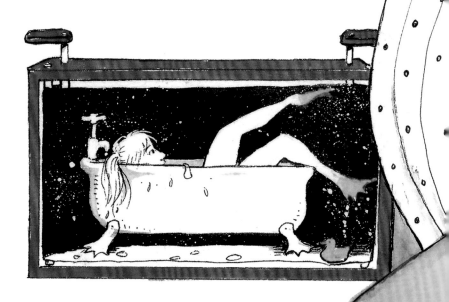

Until one night, he forgot to lock the chest.

Swan Girl dressed in her clothes and flapped her arms, and oh how they ached, for her muscles had wasted to string. She flapped and she ran and she flew into the air, over the moon and away with her sisters, free as a bird.

Next time you see a swan, look closely, it may be Swan Girl, *Y Ferch Alarch*.

The Green Man

Welsh Romany storytellers began their tales by saying 'Choiya', 'Boots', and the audience replied, '**Xolova**', 'Socks'. So let's try it.

Choiya!

Xolova!

There was once a miller called Jack, who ground the corn to make the flour to bake the bread to fill the empty bellies of the people of Wales. One day, a man walks into the mill. Nothing strange in that except this man is **green** from head to toe. Skin the colour of **limes**, hair of **grass**, and trousers of **broccoli**.

'I am the **Green Man** of No One's Land. Jack, if you can find my castle in a year and a day, it is yours, but if you fail, I will chop off your head.'

Jack likes a challenge, and he thinks a year and a day is enough time to find a big green castle. After all, he once climbed a beanstalk and fought a giant. So, he agrees, and the **Green Man** vanishes.

Jack returns to his milling, spring turns to summer and autumn leads to winter, and he remembers he likes his head on his shoulders rather than rolling around on the floor. He saddles his horse and gallops through the snow till he meets an old woman and asks if she knows where the **Green Man** lives?

'No, but if a quarter of the world's birds know, then I'll know in the morning.'

The old woman climbs a ladder onto her cottage roof, blows a horn and a quarter of the world's birds fly in. There are parrots, hummingbirds and red cardinals, but none know where the **Green Man** lives.

'Jack,' says the old woman, 'Place this ball of wool between your horse's ears and she'll take you to my older sister. She may know where the **Green Man** lives.'

Jack gallops through the snow till he comes to the old woman's older sister's cottage and asks if she knows where the **Green Man** lives.

'No, but if half the world's birds know, then you will know in the morning.'

The old woman climbs onto the roof, blows a horn and half the world's birds fly in. There are herons, flamingos and spoonbills, but none know where the **Green Man** lives.

'Jack,' says the old woman, 'Place this ball of wool between your horse's ears and she'll take you to my even older sister.'

Jack gallops to the old woman's older sister's even older sister's cottage, but she doesn't know where the **Green Man** lives.

In the morning, all the birds in the whole world fly in. Vultures, falcons, hawks and a kakapo, a flightless parrot from Aotearoa.

Then Eagle flies down. The King of the Welsh birds.

'Where have you been, lazy bird?' asks the old woman.

'Having breakfast with the **Green Man** in his castle in No One's Land.'

'Jack,' says the old woman, 'Follow Eagle to the **Green Man**'s castle.'

Eagle leads Jack to a lake where three swans remove their wings and feathers and out step three girls, who swim in the water. Eagle tells Jack to take the third girl's feathers, for she is the **Green Man's Youngest Daughter**.

Youngest Daughter tells Jack that if he returns her clothes, she will take him to her father. She dresses and, with Jack on her back, she swims into the mist towards a great mossy green castle.

The **Green Man** says, 'Jack? I was so looking forward to chopping off your head. But you're not a bright boy. Which of my daughters has helped you?'

Jack says nothing.

'That will cost you three tasks, Jack! First, clean my barn,' and the **Green Man** gives Jack a shovel and opens the barn door. It's piled high with **cachu** (poo). Jack throws a steaming shovel full out the window, and three come back and hit him splat in the face. He throws down the shovel and has a tantrum.

Youngest Daughter appears, 'Jack, stop crying. Go and clean yourself up.'

When Jack returns, the stable is spotless.

The **Green Man** says, 'Jack, and I was so looking forward to chopping off your head. Which of my daughters has helped you?'

Jack says nothing.

'Jack, your second task. In the middle of the lake is a glass mountain. On the top is the nest of the rarest bird in the world. Bring me her egg.'

Jack stands at the edge of the lake, wondering how to climb the mountain when **Youngest Daughter** removes her shoe, wishes it into a boat and sails Jack across the water.

When they reach the mountain, **Youngest Daughter** transforms into a white ladder, Jack climbs to the top, takes the egg, and as he steps on the last rung, there's a crack, and when she turns into a girl, her little finger is broken.

Jack gives the egg to the **Green Man**. 'Jack, I was so looking forward to chopping off your head. Your third task. Three swans will fly three times around the castle. Tell me which is my **Youngest Daughter**.'

All the swans are as white as snow with yellow beaks and orange feet. But one has a broken wing feather.

Jack points, 'There is your youngest daughter.'

The **Green Man** was so looking forward to chopping off Jack's head, but he hands over the keys to his castle.

Jack gives the keys to **Youngest Daughter** and returns to grinding corn to make the flour to bake the bread to fill the bellies of the people of Wales.

And **Youngest Daughter** returns the egg to the nest on the glass mountain and invites all the birds of the world to make their nests in her Green Castle.

Choiya!
Xolova!

The Horse that pooped gold

Choiya!
Xolova!

There was once a poor man, a travelling man, a Welsh Romany, who had little money and nowhere to keep the little he had. He couldn't hide it in the house because he didn't have one, so he kept his money in his horse. He mixed a few coins in with her oats and hay, and whenever he wanted to spend some, he waited till the horse did a poo. Then he rolled up his sleeves and wiggled his fingers around in the poo till he found the coins.

One day, the poor man was wiping a coin on his shirt when a rich man passed by and saw what he thought was a horse that pooped gold. So, he offered loads of money to buy the horse. But the poor man said, 'No! Rosie and I have been together since I was a boy. We have travelled all over Wales, through Scotland and Ireland, across Europe and around the World. No! I'll never part with my dearest friend. Keep your money.'

So, the rich man offered a little more and the deal was done, leaving the poor man with loads of money and nowhere to keep it.

The rich man took the horse home, fed her the finest oats and hay, and waited till she did a poo. He put on a pair of white silk gloves and approached the steaming pile, and it was hot and smelly, and as the sweat poured from his brow, he plunged his hands in and wiggled his fingers around and what do you think he found?

Nothing!

So, he took the horse back to the poor man and complained that it didn't poo gold. The poor man asked, 'What do you feed your horse?'

The rich man replied, 'Only the finest oats and hay.'

'Well, there you are,' said the poor man. 'To get gold from your horse, you have to feed her gold.'

So the poor man was a little richer and the rich man a little poorer. And isn't that how life ought to be?

Choiya!
Xolova!

Wild Pony

Wild Pony lived in the forest as free as the birds. She ate as many apples as she wanted, rolled in the dry leaves whenever she could and leapt in the air just because she felt like it.

One morning, she was galloping through the trees when she found herself at the edge of the forest. She looked over the fence and there was a green clover meadow with a stream of silver water and an old piebald carthorse, who had iron shoes on his hooves.

Wild Pony had a thought. Why was she living in a gloomy forest with only muddy water to drink, when she could live in a green clover meadow and drink from a silver stream. And she wanted iron shoes like Carthorse. Pink ones.

Wild Pony snorted, pawed the ground, shook her shaggy mane, leapt over the fence and landed with a splat at Carthorse's feet.

Carthorse looked puzzled, 'What are you doing, you crazy Wild Pony?'

'I want to live in a green meadow and eat clover and drink water from a silver stream and have pink shoes on my hooves, like you.'

Carthorse shook his plaited mane, 'And I want to live free in the forest and eat apples and run barefoot like you, and never have to haul wagons full of timber again.'

At that moment, the farmer placed a bridle round Wild Pony's head, hitched her to a wagon, and she found herself hauling fence posts cut from the trees in the forest where she once roamed free.

And she dreamed of eating apples, rolling in the dry leaves and leaping into the air, just because she could.

You see, the grass isn't always greener on the other side of the fence.

Though there's no harm in dreaming.

Ceffyl Dŵr

One evening, Megan sat on the beach below St Illtyd's Church waiting for her Grandfather to sail his boat into Oxwich Bay with his lobsterpots. The white waves crashed onto the sand, yet there was no wind. As she watched, one huge wave leapt out of the water, grew a head, legs and a tail, galloped along the beach like a wild pony from Cefn Bryn, jumped over the rocks and disappeared through the trees towards the church.

Megan ran to the churchyard gate, and there, among the gravestones, stood a white horse, glowing in the moonlight. It pranced on its hind legs, blew steam from its nostrils and shook raindrops from its shaggy, white mane. It snorted and galloped towards her, yet it made no sound, and time slowed to a trot. Megan noticed its hooves pointed backwards and didn't touch the ground.

Megan opened the churchyard gate and the ghost horse ran silently past her into the mist. Her clothes and hair were soaked with seawater.

A light shone by the side of the church and there was Grandfather holding a lantern and a box of lobsters. He dried his granddaughter with a woollen blanket, and as they walked back to their shack in the woods, she told him about the white Water Horse.

Grandfather sat by the fire and she curled up on his lap as he spoke, 'Megan, you saw a Ceffyl Dŵr, a Water Horse. Sometimes, when there are storms out at sea, the waves leave the water and you can hear the sound of thundering hooves on the sand as they gallop across Oxwich Bay.

'Some folks say they get up to mischief. They give rides to fishermen, then fly into the air and drop the poor rider hundreds of miles from home. But I met a Ceffyl Dŵr once, and it saved my life. It was a December full moon with snow in the air, and I was about to take the boat to check the lobsterpots off the Three Cliffs when I saw it, white and ghostly, shaking its shaggy mane. I knew I had to follow it. It led me home, then it leapt over the roof and vanished. That night a storm blew out at sea and many boats were lost. I wouldn't be here to tell you the story if I'd gone out to sea that night, but the Ceffyl Dŵr saved me from drowning. And it saved me again tonight.'

Grandfather looked down. The Ceffyl Dŵr had sent Megan to sleep.

Donkey's Ears

March ab Meirchion of Castellmarch, Lord of Pen Llŷn, wanted someone to cut his hair. However, no one applied for the job because March had a habit of ordering his executioner to chop off his hairdressers' heads. So, his hair grew longer and longer until he piled it up like a beehive. A wren nested in it.

A girl from Aberdaron applied for the job, even though she couldn't cut her own bangs straight. However, she had a pair of sparkly pink scissors and the silver tongue of a storyteller, and she knew she could talk her way out of trouble. So, she became March's official hairdresser.

On her first day at work, March ordered, 'A little off the sides but leave it high on top'. As her sparkly pink scissors clipped, the hairdresser discovered the Lord of Pen Llŷn had a secret. Hidden beneath his hair were two long, furry donkey's ears.

The quick-thinking hairdresser realised she might lose her head, so she started talking to hide her fear. 'Would you like a pink streak? Mohawk? Curtains? Double buns? Spikes? A mullet? No, not a mullet. I'm good at bangs. A pony tail?'

'Are you trying to tell me something, hairdresser?'

'Nay, your Hairyness.'

'Did you say "Neigh"?'

'No, your Shaggyness, I said, "Hey"!'

'Hay?'

The hairdresser pretended to be deaf, 'Sorry, I'm a little hoarse.'

Like all good storytellers, she knew when to stop, and she vanished before March called for the axe.

But the secret was too big.

It nibbled away at her and made her belly ache like a mouse who'd eaten too much cheese. She had to tell someone before she burst. So, she whispered her secret to the River Daron, 'March has donkey's ears'.

The river giggled.

In the spring, reeds grew on the riverbank and a travelling piper cut one to play at March's birthday party. That evening, at Castellmarch, he raised the new pipe to his lips, but as the tune swirled through the reed, something weird happened. The pipe began to sing, over and over, 'March has donkey's ears.'

'March has donkey's ears', louder and louder, 'March has donkey's ears'.

A deathly silence settled over the court. The piper gulped and held his neck.

Then someone giggled, followed by a chuckle, and soon everyone was laughing, big belly laughs. March turned red with rage and ordered them to stop, or … and he drew his hand across his throat.

The hairdresser stepped forward, 'March, why are you so embarrassed? You have furry ears we can only dream of. Your hearing must be amazing. And I bet they keep you warm at night? I'd love hairy ears like yours.'

Well, March thought for a moment, then he giggled, and his giggle became a laugh, and everyone on Pen Llŷn laughed with him, not at him, and from that day he wore his hair down to show off his long, furry ears.

You see, it takes a storyteller to teach someone they aren't an ass. And they're all good storytellers in Aberdaron.

Mari Lwyd

Myra is standing in the front bedroom window of her aunt's house on Margaret Street, her green eyes shining beneath her black fringe as she stares at the falling snow. The people of Cei Newydd scurry past, their breath freezing in the night air. Myra opens her mouth to speak but Mam tells her to hush or she'll be put to bed in the back room. For this is the night when the Ghost Horse will visit.

Mari Lwyd – Grey Mary.

Myra hears singing, and there it is, outside Bristol House, a horse skull decorated with ribbons and roses of yellow and red, held by a mysterious figure draped in a white sheet, with legs and shoes sticking out beneath. Behind are masked characters dressed in animal skins, children wearing squirrel tail hats, all chanting rhymes asking for food and drink.

'Mae Mari Lwyd lawen yn dyfod i'ch trigfan,
O, peidiwch a bod yn sych ac anniddan.
O, peidiwch yn wir, mae'r amser yn wan,
Rhowch law yn eich poced a gwnewch eich rhan.'

They turn into Tin Pan Alley and stop outside Manchester House and then they are below Myra's window.

The ghost horse clacks its jaws and a tooth falls into the snow. A small, masked figure picks it up, rolls it into a snowball and throws it at Mari. An arm reaches out from beneath the sheet and hurls the snowball back at the child.

'*Wel dyma ni'n dwad, gyfeillion diniwad,*
I mofyn am gennad a ganu.
O tapwch y faril, gollyngwch y rhigl,
Na fyddwch yn gynnil i'r Fari.'

Myra follows Mam downstairs. Mam opens the door and sings sweetly back to the Mari party, offers them a tray of cakes and a jug of plum and rhubarb wine and tells them not to trash anything or there'll be trouble.

Myra asks who's under the sheet, and Mam whispers, 'William Evans', one of Ceinewydd's many shoemakers. Myra peeps into the sheets and glimpses William's hairy head.

William asks, 'Elmira. Is your dad home?'

'No, he's out at sea in Rosina.'

'Ask him to bring me a couple of herring, and I'll fix the holes in your boots.'

Everyone shouts, '*Blwyddyn Newydd Dda*!' and Mari floats away into the cold mist towards the New Year.

Mae'r amser yn galed, a'r tywydd yn oer,
A'r hodion ynrhynnu dan lewyrch y lloer
Dim bwyd yn y cwpwrdd na thân yn y tŷ'
Ar noswaith oer rewllyd, dim cysur y sy.

Myra doesn't think it weird that she had a conversation with a ghost horse. She was born at midnight on *Calan Gaeaf*, when the veil between this world and the otherworld is at its thinnest, when spirits pass through and we remember those who walked the land before us. Myra is a child of two worlds.

The Red Bandits

I n an old damp cottage in Dinas Mawddwy lived a young
woman with her baby, a cow and some chickens. She
lived off milk and eggs and gathered sheep's wool from
the brambles and barbed wire to spin into clothes for her
baby. Until, one morning, her cow and chickens were
missing, and she knew they had been taken by the Gwylliaid
Cochion, bandits with flaming red hair who robbed
travellers, ransacked farmhouses and hid in the mountains.

That night she stuffed scythe blades up the chimney to
stop the bandits climbing down. She sat by the fire singing
a lullaby to her baby, when a little old lady walked in, peered
through bottle-bottom glasses and dropped a bag of coins
on the table.

'What will you give me if I give you this gold?' asked the little old lady.

The woman was feeling drowsy in the heat of the fire, but she heard herself say, 'I'd give you anything for a bag of gold.'

The little old lady licked her thumb with a raspberry tongue, placed the top joint against the woman's thumb, and said, 'Give me your baby!'

'You're crazy! I'll never give you my baby. Keep your gold.'

'A deal with the tylwyth teg can't be broken, but each night for three nights you'll have three chances to guess my name. If you fail, your baby will be mine.'

The woman blurted out, 'Megan, Myfi, Mari?'

The little old lady cackled and danced away, as old ladies do in fairy tales.

The woman thought she was dreaming, but the following night the little old lady returned and asked for her name.

'Ceri, Caryl, Cerys?'

The old lady danced away, cackling and licking her raspberry tongue.

The woman wrapped her baby in a shawl and ran through the forest, muttering names, 'Gwennan, Gwenllian, Georgia?'

As she stood by the banks of the Dyfi, she heard singing, and there in a clearing in the trees was the little old lady, dancing around her spinning wheel, surrounded by wagtails who flicked their tails while she chanted, 'Sigl-di-gwt. Sigl-di-gwt. Sigl-di-gwt is my name.'

Sigl-di-gwt is Welsh for wagtail.

The woman couldn't believe her ears. She turned and ran home.

That night the little old lady came, 'Well what's my name?'

'Siani?'

The old lady cackled, 'No!'

'Siriol?'

The old lady reached out towards the baby with bony fingers.

'No!'

'Would it be Sigl-di-gwt?'

Megan Myfi Mari

The old lady turned red, steam poured from her ears, spit from her mouth, green goo from her nose, she leapt up and down, stamped her foot three times, broke the floorboards and vanished through the hole, never to be seen again.

With all the gold, the woman bought some more scythes to stuff up the chimney to keep out the Cochion Gwylliaid.

A few days later, she found her old cow and a few chickens hiding in a tree.

The bandits had returned them.

Arthur

A poor shepherd lad from Glynneath sat beneath an old, gnarled hazel tree on Craig y Ddinas dreaming of how to make his fortune when all he had was a small flock of scraggy sheep. His dream told him to sell them at Smithfield Market in London, where they had more money than he did. So, he cut a stick from the tree, wrapped his few belongings in a red, spotted handkerchief, and walked along the drovers' road with the Welsh shepherds and a few farm girls who hoped to find work in the big smoke.

Later that evening, he stood on London Bridge counting his money and found he hardly had enough to buy a bag of chips, never mind a train ticket home to Port Talbot. He wondered whether to stay in London and become a poet, when a stranger approached and said, 'That's a fine stick. Is it from the old, gnarled hazel tree on Craig y Ddinas?'

'How did you know?' asked the lad.

'I dreamed I would meet you on London Bridge and together we would find gold beneath that tree.'

The lad's eyes lit up. This man was as gnarled and twisted as the stick. He looked like a cunning man. A *dyn hysbys*.

So, they walked home to Wales and climbed to the top of Craig-y-Ddinas, where the stranger gave the lad a shovel and told him to dig. There was a clang, and they lifted a stone to find a flight of steps. The lad climbed down and followed a rope along a corridor to a stagnant cave that smelled of sweaty men who hadn't washed in a thousand years.

And there they were, clutching swords and shields, sat at a great oak table piled with gold coins, shaking the spider webs with their snoring. Hanging above a giant man with red-plaited hair was a bell. The lad knew this was King Arthur, waiting for the bell to ring to save his people from their latest mess.

The lad filled his pockets with coins and followed the rope up the steps into the Welsh night air. He gave the gold to the stranger and returned for more, but this time, his elbow caught the bell, and there was a **CLANG!** The smelly warriors awoke, shook the dust and fleas from their beards, surrounded the lad and poked him with their rusty, iron swords.

Arthur boomed, '*A ydyw hi'n ddydd?*'

The King clearly hadn't brushed his teeth in a millennium because his breath smelled like a silent fart, but the lad kept cool, 'No, my King, go back to sleep. I'll wake you when the day comes.'

Arthur and his warriors closed their eyes, laid their heads on their chainmail arms, and soon they were snoring like the sleeping beauties they weren't.

The lad returned to the surface with empty pockets to find the stranger had vanished with the gold. He turned round to see the gnarled, old tree disappear before his eyes. And there were his sheep, laughing at him for being so greedy.

The Faithful Hound

Gelert lay curled up by the fire in Llywelyn and Johanna's forest lodge at Aber, where he protected their new-born baby from wolves. His nose twitched as he dreamed of chasing a wolf through the trees and scratching himself on fallen branches. No wolf dared challenge him, for he was stronger than a lion and faster than a tiger, yet gentle as a lamb and whiter than a swan.

One day, Llywelyn and Johanna tucked their baby safely into his cradle by the fire and rode through the forest with their faithful wolfhound. Gelert's ears pricked at every sound and his red tongue tasted the air, until suddenly he stopped. Something was wrong. He hadn't seen a wolf all day.

Gelert galloped back to the lodge to find the door unlatched. He crept inside and there, towering over the cradle, was an enormous wolf with a shaggy mane, dribbling and drooling and dreaming of dinner. Gelert leapt in front of the cradle and knocked it over to hide the baby, and he growled at the wolf.

Llywelyn and Johanna followed
Gelert back to the lodge and found the
wolfhound lying beside the upturned cradle,
licking blood from his fur. Gelert jumped to his
feet and wagged his tail when he saw them and waited
to be fussed. He watched as Llywelyn drew his sword and
raised his arm. Time slowed.

Gelert lay down by the fire to lick his wound. His nose
twitched and he dreamed of racing through the trees and
scratching himself on fallen branches. Then his eyes closed.
Only then did Llywelyn and Johanna realise that Gelert
had saved their baby and fought off the wolf. They
remembered the saying, 'As sorry as the man who killed
his wolfhound'.

Gelert's grave lies close to the river in the village named
after him, Beddgelert. Though some mischievous people
will tell you this story was invented by the landlord of
the Goat Hotel to attract visitors to the town, but it's a
much older tale. So old, it may even have been told by
Llywelyn, Prince of Wales, himself.

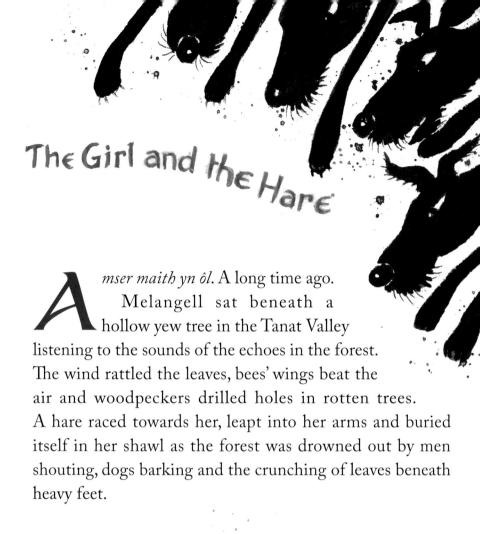

The Girl and the Hare

A*mser maith yn ôl.* A long time ago. Melangell sat beneath a hollow yew tree in the Tanat Valley listening to the sounds of the echoes in the forest. The wind rattled the leaves, bees' wings beat the air and woodpeckers drilled holes in rotten trees. A hare raced towards her, leapt into her arms and buried itself in her shawl as the forest was drowned out by men shouting, dogs barking and the crunching of leaves beneath heavy feet.

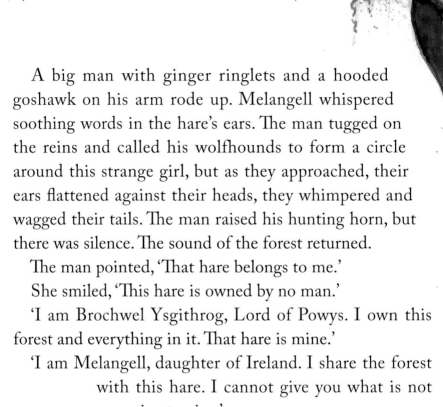

A big man with ginger ringlets and a hooded goshawk on his arm rode up. Melangell whispered soothing words in the hare's ears. The man tugged on the reins and called his wolfhounds to form a circle around this strange girl, but as they approached, their ears flattened against their heads, they whimpered and wagged their tails. The man raised his hunting horn, but there was silence. The sound of the forest returned.

The man pointed, 'That hare belongs to me.'

She smiled, 'This hare is owned by no man.'

'I am Brochwel Ysgithrog, Lord of Powys. I own this forest and everything in it. That hare is mine.'

'I am Melangell, daughter of Ireland. I share the forest with this hare. I cannot give you what is not mine to give.'

'You live in my forest? Then I own you, too,' Brochwel smirked.

'I fled marriage in Ireland. I cannot be owned by one so in love with himself.'

Brochwel removed the goshawk's hood and launched the bird into the air. It circled above Melangell as she closed her eyes, moved her lips silently and held out her hand. The goshawk swooped down and landed on her arm. She stroked its feathers. Its claws didn't scratch her skin.

Brochwel called the bird but it refused to fly to him. His horse stepped back and snorted. The dogs retreated. He had lost control.

'Where do you live?'

'In this hollow yew tree. That rock is my bed. I sleep beneath a quilt of leaves and roses. Thorns protect me.'

Brochwel thought for a moment, 'Then I give you permission to live here if you look after the forest for me. I won't pay you, though.'

'Birdsong has more value to me than money,' and Melangell launched the goshawk into the air. It circled above Brochwel and flew off through the trees.

A shiver passed through his body. He had never met anyone who spoke to the birds and cared nothing for gold.

He had no words. He nodded, called his dogs and rode away, with the hare snapping at their heels like a wolfhound. For the first time in his life he understood that he was powerless in the face of this girl. He felt something new. A desire to help the forest.

This all happened a very long time ago, yet the hollow yew trees are still there in the Tanat Valley, standing guard over the little church at Pennant Melangell, where the story of the girl and the hare will always be told.

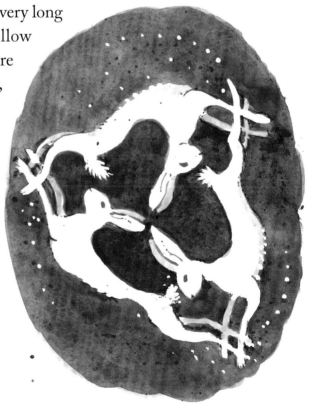

The Lady of Ogmore

A long time ago, when the Normans ruled Wales, a **Welshman** was brought before the Lord of Ogmore and accused of poaching.

'What were you doing on my land?'

'It's not your land.'

'Of course it's my land.'

'Did you buy it, then?'

'I inherited it from my father.'

'Where did he get it from?'

'From his father.'

'And where did your grandfather get it from?'

'From his father.'

'And where did your great grandfather get it from?'

'He defeated the Welsh in battle.'

'Okay, let's arm wrestle. Winner gets the land?'

'Throw him in the dungeon.'

'Rock, paper, scissors? Scrabble? Minecraft?'

The Lord's daughter, the Lady of Ogmore, was listening.

'Papa?'

'*Oui, petite maman*?'

'Papa, can I have my birthday present now?'

'Of course, what would you like?'

'This man's freedom.'

'No, he's been poaching on my land.'

'It's not your land, Papa. This man's ancestors lived here long before we took the land from him.'

'Exactly, this is my land now.'

'The land was here before you were born and will be here after you. It's on loan to you and should be shared. Release him.'

'No.'

'I'll protest. I can scream. You know I can.'

'Please don't scream. It hurts my ears.'

The lady opened her mouth and the lord turned white.

'Alright. I will give you all the land you can walk around barefoot before the sun sets. Please don't scream.'

The Lady of Ogmore stared into her father's eyes, kicked off her sandals, and walked swiftly from Candleston to Merthyr Mawr and along the river and coast from Ewenny to Southerndown. The thorns and flints tore her feet, but she never stopped, not once, and all the while her father's soldiers followed, measuring her every step.

At the end of the day, she stared into her father's eyes again as she bandaged the cuts on her feet. The Norman lord loved his daughter, and true to his word, he gave her the land, and she in turn gave it to the poacher, who returned it to the people of Ogmore.

And the nature reserves of Ogmore are open to all the people of Wales to this day, all thanks to the lord's daughter.

The Corpse Bride

Meinir Maredydd was all dressed up as an old woman in a long, black dress with a high, lace collar, lines drawn on her face with charcoal from the fireplace and a pair of spectacles balanced on the end of her nose. Nan was tying Meinir's hair into a bun when they heard singing outside the front door at Tŷ Hen, the family farm in Nant Gwrtheyrn. Cousin Rhys had arrived to take Meinir to St Bueno's Church in Clynnog, where they were to be married.

Nan opened the door and told Rhys he'd have to find his bride-to-be first. But all he could see was a wrinkled old woman in a rocking chair by the fire. He looked for Meinir under the beds, behind the cupboards, and in the tŷ bach, but there was no sign of her.

Nan sent Rhys off to search the schoolroom, the bracken and the cliffs at Carreg y Llam. When he was out of sight, she giggled, pushed Meinir out the back door and told her to hide until Rhys found her. Or leave the Nant and run away on her own to somewhere exotic like Paris, Rome or Aberystwyth?

Rhys knew it was all meant to be fun, but still he couldn't find Meinir. He knocked on doors in Llithfaen, Llanaelhaearn and Trefor but no one had seen her. Days, weeks, months passed and still Rhys searched, his dog by his side, through rain and wind. Then, one evening, during a fierce storm, a bolt of lightning struck a hollow oak tree at the foot of Yr Eifl. The tree split open and a figure floated away.

Some said Meinir had hidden in the tree and become trapped, others that the tylwyth teg had captured her, but Nan knew it was the Curse.

Years before, three monks from Clynnog cast a spell on Y Nant. If any cousins dared to marry, the village would slowly die before being reborn. Rhys didn't believe these fairy tales. He knew Meinir was waiting for him.

This all happened a long time ago, but the lovers are still seen, walking arm in arm along the beach or flying through the air, he with long, white hair and she in a frayed wedding dress, forever the corpse bride and groom of Nant Gwrtheyrn.

And old Nan's story of the Curse? Well, the village did die, when the Nant Quarries closed in the 1950s and young people left to search for work, while their family homes fell into ruin. But this fairy tale has a happy ending, as Nan said it would.

Antur Aelhaearn, a community co-operative pottery and knitwear shop, brought work back to Llithfaen and Llanaelhaearn. Then Y Nant was reborn as the National Welsh Language Centre, now a venue for weddings, where lovers have their photos taken next to a sculpture of Meinir's oak tree.

Oh, and I'll tell you a little secret. My first job when I grew up was in Antur Aelhaearn, where I designed the drawings to go on the pottery.

Bag o' Bones

Choiya!
Xolova!

A poor scraggy lad called Bones was looking for work down by the harbour to earn a few pennies, when a hairy sea captain said, 'Ahoy, Bag o' Bones, I've a job for you on the *Barti Ddu*, swabbing the deck, cleaning out the crow's nest and looking after the ship's parrot.'

Captain gave him a mop, 'Bag o' Bones, swab the deck, and be quick about it!'

But Bones was so slow that Captain slapped him on the back to hurry him along and he fell to pieces. There were ribs and funnybones scattered all over the deck. Captain went to fetch a sweeping brush, but when he returned, Bones was all back together again.

Captain told Bones, 'Clean out the crow's nest.'

So, Bones climbed up the mast but fell off the rigging and landed in a heap of thighbones and backbones on the deck. Captain brushed the bones into the sea and went to his cabin to teach his parrot rude words, and there was Bones in the doorway, all back together again.

Captain told Bones, 'Look after the parrot while I go on a rumbustification.'

Did I tell you he was a pirate captain?

But the parrot pecked Bones apart and Captain threw the skull into the hold and stamped the rest of the bones into dust. A moment later, there was Bones, all back together again, grinning like a cartoon skellington.

On they sailed, until they came to an island, where the crew went ashore to do some pillaging. Captain took Bones to a lonely spot and knocked him into pieces, burned his ribs, buried his backbones, scattered his legbones, left his armbones in a recycling bag and stamped the rest into dust. Then he ordered the crew to stop pillaging and set sail. When he set foot on deck, there was Bones at the wheel, grinning.

So, Captain said, 'Bag o' Bones, here's my hat, cutlass and parrot. You can be Captain now.' And he jumped overboard and swam back to the island.

And that's how Bones found work as a Pirate Captain, just like Barti Ddu.

Choiya!
Xolova!

The Coal Giant

A mean Giant lived in the forest of Gilfach Fargoed. He tore down all the trees to make a bonfire to keep himself warm, while the poor people of Rhymney were so cold you could hear their teeth chattering in Merthyr. And that wasn't the worst of it. The Giant roasted the people on his bonfire and ate them for dinner. He was one bad giant, and the people agreed he had to go.

A boy who spoke the language of the birds went to see the wise old Owl who lived in an ancient oak tree at Pencoed Fawr. The Owl agreed to help, since the Giant had been snacking on birds, too. She summoned all the Owls of Rhymney, the Tawny, Barn, Little, Short-eared and Long-eared, and they hatched a plan.

The Tawny Owls carved a huge bow and arrow from the branches of an old apple tree where the Giant met his girlfriend, the Witch of Rhymney.

The Barn Owls dug a deep pit beneath the tree.

The Little Owls covered the pit with sticks.

The Short-eared Owls covered the sticks with leaves.

The Long-eared Owls pulled back the bow.

And they all hid in the apple tree and waited.

In the morning, the Giant went to the apple tree to meet his girlfriend and catch some children to fry for breakfast with mushrooms. As he stepped on the sticks, the Owls fired the arrow, which squished through the Giant's heart, the sticks broke beneath his feet and down he tumbled into the pit.

The Owls filled in the pit with earth and flew away before he woke up.

One day, the Witch was searching for the Giant when she spotted a piece of dark, shiny crystal beneath the apple tree. She took it home and found it turned her hand black. '*Ych a fi!*' she shouted, and threw it on her tiny fire. It burned for hours and she sat in front of it in her underwear warming her toes.

The people of the forest wanted fire too, so they dug beneath the apple tree and found the Giant had turned into dark, shiny crystal. They burned him on their fires and called him, Y Cawr Glo, the **Coal Giant**.

When the Witch realised they were burning her lover, she cursed the tree till its apples turned sour. That was the first crab apple.

A wealthy man saw there was money to be made from coal, so he built a pithead round the apple tree and sold the black crystal to the poor people of Rhymney, until one day all of the **Coal Giant** had been burned.

Teeth chattered once again, until the hidden people of the forest realised they had to find a new Giant of Rhymney to keep themselves warm as toast.

And that's why we now have –
    the Wind Giant,
        the Sea Giant,
            and the Sun Giant.

The Ferny Man

On Calan Mai, when the veil between this world and the otherworld was at its thinnest, ghosts walked on the Garth Mountain. Eira often saw them, with their curly hair and dark eyes, as they haunted the five Bronze Age burial mounds and the Lan Colliery. They smiled as they passed her. Some of them were small, children who walked up the mountain one day and never returned. They were caught in an explosion at the colliery, and still wander the mountain to this day. And there are older spirits, hazy and misty, those who live forever in the burial mounds. None of them were scary, although there were other spirits who weren't friendly ghosts.

It was the morning after Calan Mai, and Eira was at home in Tonteg making omelettes for breakfast, when she heard a voice.

'Can I have one? I'm starvin'.'

The omelette on the end of Eira's fork stopped in front of her open mouth. She looked around. There was no one there. Was this one of the Garth ghosts?

The voice spoke again. 'Sorry I was late home last night, love.'

'Dad, is that you?'

'I didn't want to wake you when I got back from Cardiff, so I slept on the sofa.'

'Dad, I can't see you. Where are you?'

'I'm right here,' said Dad.

Eira reached out and touched his shoulder.

Dad explained, 'I was walking home over the Garth, wishing it was a hill 'cos it would be easier to climb than a mountain.'

'Dad, the Garth is a hill, even though we call it a mountain. Folks say that our ancestors built the burial mounds on the top so it would be 1000ft high, and therefore a mountain not a hill. But it's rubbish. It was in a film.'

'It's still steep to climb, especially after a night out with the boys. Then when I got to the top, the air filled with dust, and I couldn't see my hands.'

'What time was it when you reached the summit?' asked Eira.

'Around midnight.'

'Dad, at midnight on Calan Mai, the fern seed on the Garth ripens and if you brush against it, you become invisible. You're covered in it. I can see it shimmering around you.'

'What? I'm a ghost! I knew climbing that mountain would kill me stone dead.'

'You're not a ghost, Dad, and it's a hill. I'll be able to see you again when the fern seeds drop off.'

'Righto,' said Dad, 'Let's have some fun.'

So Eira and Invisible Dad spent the day in Cardiff, and Dad had free rides on the Pleasure Beach on Barry Island, free entry into Techniquest, free shows at Chapter Arts Centre, and just as he ran down the middle of Queen Street in the nude, his visibility returned.

Just think. What would you do in Cardiff if you were invisible?

Moon Girl

Y Brenin Llwyd, the Grey King, was a cold mist that sat on top of Snowdon. It was so thick that the passengers on the little mountain railway couldn't see the tips of their noses. They complained to the driver that they had paid to see the sunset from the top of the mountain, but nothing would move the grumpy old Grey King from his throne.

Morfudd had climbed the mountain rather than catch the train because she liked to walk slowly. As she neared the summit, she hung her backpack on a low branch of a twisted thorn tree, took a drink from her flask and said, 'Brenin Llwyd. *Mynd i ffwrdd!*'

A strong wind appeared from nowhere and the Grey King was blown clean off his throne. The sky cleared, the sun shone and there, peeping through the branches of the thorn tree, was the crescent moon.

Morfudd ran to the summit to photograph the last of the sunset, but realised she'd left her phone in her bag. She ran back to the thorn tree, but her backpack had vanished.

She looked up and there was her bag, hanging from the tip of the crescent moon. The moon grew arms and legs and transformed into Y Ferch Lleuad, the girl with moonlight for hair. Moon Girl reached out her hand and gave the backpack to Morfudd, who ran to the top of the mountain to take a phone-photo before the sun set.

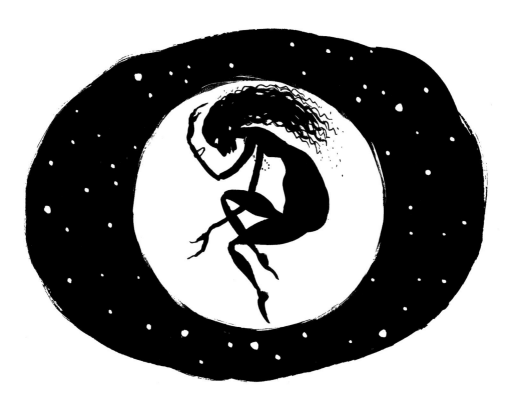

Moon Girl grinned.

As Morfudd walked back
down the mountain, Moon Girl lit
her path. The little train overtook her, full of
passengers who never saw the Snowdon sunset,
the grumpy Grey King or the mischievous Moon Girl.
All they saw was mist.

For you have to walk slowly to see magic like that.

Cadwaladr and the Goats

Long ago, before Wales was full of sheep, farmers kept goats. They were wild, shaggy creatures, who wandered over the mountains and rolled in the mud until their straggly beards were sticky with thistles and burdocks.

Cadwaladr the Goatkeeper decided to smarten up his goats by combing their beards. But the goats liked being scruffy, so they ran away, all apart from Gwenno, who loved having her beard combed till it was as smooth as silk.

'Oh, I love my Gwenno's beard,' said Cadwaladr as he wove it into plaits.

The other goats brayed and grumbled because they thought Gwenno looked like one of those fancy new breeds. What were they called? Sheep! They told Gwenno she ought to have a straggly beard like a good goat.

One day she vanished, and when she hadn't returned by twilight, Cadwaladr went to search for her. He found her on a ledge high on the mountain.

'Gwenno, *tyd yma*. Let me plait your beard.'

But Gwenno said nothing.

'Gwenno, *tyd*. I will weave flowers in your beard.'

But Gwenno was crying.

Cadwaladr threw a stone to frighten Gwenno into returning to him, but she slipped and tumbled down into the gorge.

Cadwaladr clambered down after her and laid her head in his lap. He stroked her beard, she licked his hand and as the moon rose, he looked down, and Gwenno was a young woman with a silky-smooth beard.

She spoke to him with such a sweet, bleating voice. She took his hand in her hoof and they climbed out of the gorge. And there were all his goats, pawing at the ground and snorting. When they saw Gwenno had turned into an ugly human, one big hairy billy-goat pointed his horns, charged at Cadwaladr and butted him down into the gorge. When Cadwaladr hit the ground, he opened his eyes and looked around for Gwenno, but there were no goats to be seen. Only sheep, as far as the eye could see.

That's why the wild goats in Wales today avoid people. Except in Llandudno.

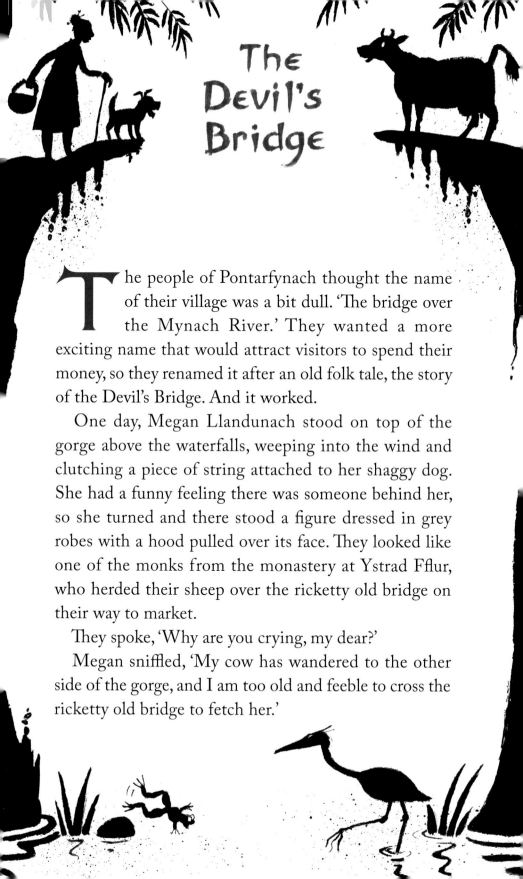

The Devil's Bridge

The people of Pontarfynach thought the name of their village was a bit dull. 'The bridge over the Mynach River.' They wanted a more exciting name that would attract visitors to spend their money, so they renamed it after an old folk tale, the story of the Devil's Bridge. And it worked.

One day, Megan Llandunach stood on top of the gorge above the waterfalls, weeping into the wind and clutching a piece of string attached to her shaggy dog. She had a funny feeling there was someone behind her, so she turned and there stood a figure dressed in grey robes with a hood pulled over its face. They looked like one of the monks from the monastery at Ystrad Fflur, who herded their sheep over the ricketty old bridge on their way to market.

They spoke, 'Why are you crying, my dear?'

Megan sniffled, 'My cow has wandered to the other side of the gorge, and I am too old and feeble to cross the ricketty old bridge to fetch her.'

Megan wiped a dewdrop from her nose and looked at the monk's feet. They were cloven. Like a goat. He was no monk.

'Don't worry,' said the Devil, for it was them, 'I will build you a beautiful new bridge, if you give me the soul of the first living creature that crosses over.'

The Devil twirled their beard and thought, 'These old women from Pontarfynach are so easy to fool.'

Before Megan could blink an eye, the gorge was spanned by a slightly less ricketty bridge. The Devil carved their name into the wood, as carpenters do, and proudly showed it to Megan, expecting praise, a fresh human soul and organic beefburgers for dinner. Instead, the crafty old woman pulled a stale loaf from her pocket, threw it across the gorge, released the dog from its string and shouted, 'Fetch!' The dog chased the bread across the bridge to the other side.

The Devil let out a howl that froze the River Mynach and vanished, leaving behind the soul of the shabby dog and resolving never again to mess with old women from Pont Diafol, the Devil's Bridge.

The Elephant of Tregaron

Long ago, George Batty's Travelling Menagerie rolled into Tregaron on its way from the South Bank in London to the fairs in Aberystwyth and Cardigan. It was an old-fashioned circus, with animal acts we wouldn't see nowadays. There was Lena, the bareback horse rider, Thomas, the lion tamer, Madame Frederica and her amazing performing dog, a magnificent mandrill, a young Russian bear, and a seven-year-old Indian elephant called Rajah. It was raining old ladies with sticks as the wagons formed a circle outside the Talbot Hotel.

A curly haired Tregaron lad was wondering whether he should release the animals from their cages when Mr Batty dropped a coin in his hand and pointed at the elephant, who was wobbling from side to side. The lad knew the elephant was sick with fever, so he led her to the stable, gave her fresh hay and straw, washed her leathery skin to cool her and sang lullabies in Welsh to calm her. In the morning, he went to see if Mr Batty might give him more coins, but the Travelling Menagerie had rolled on, leaving behind a sickly elephant.

Ask anyone what happened next and they'll tell you the elephant was buried at the back of the Talbot Hotel. Or under the car park. Or was dragged over the hill towards Bont.

Or it was made into a giant bowl of cawl. Though a recent archaeological dig at the back of the Talbot found … nothing!

That's because the elephant was still alive. The kind folk of Tregaron kept her warm and cooled her fever with spring water, while the curly haired lad ran to a cottage in the hills to fetch his Nan. She was a *dynes hysbys*. She made charms and potions that could cure anything but rain. And she could fly inside the minds of animals.

The lad told her about the elephant and she filled her bag with bottles and powders, and within the blink of a crow's eye she flew to the stable. The elephant thrashed its trunk from side to side. Nan shook her arms and went into a trance, just like the old soothsayers. Her body crumpled, the lad caught her, but her mind was inside the great, grey body. She soothed it with gentle words and slowed its heartbeat till it dreamed of flying through the night sky.

The lad carried Nan home and placed her in the old mahogany rocking chair by the fire, wrapped a shawl around her shoulders and left her a drink for when she woke up, purely for medicinal purposes. Then he ran back to the stable, where the elephant had calmed. He led her groggily out of town to Nan's cottage to live a happy life, free from the cages of Batty's Travelling Menagerie.

In the morning, the people found the stable empty, and when Mr Batty called to collect his elephant on his way home to London, the people of Tregaron told him, 'It's buried at the back of the Talbot!' And the lad grew up with the finest playmate any child could wish for.

And that's how the tale of the elephant of Tregaron began, but maybe you have another idea?

The Tale of Taliesin

Imagine you'd never had a single thought in your whole life. Your mind was blank. Like gazing at the night sky but with no stars. Well, this was Gwion as he wandered through the forest by Llyn Tegid. He never noticed his feet were wet when he stood in the lake. He didn't feel pain when he fell out of trees, which he often did. He couldn't think of answers to anything but did as he was told. That was why the nice lady he met in the forest gave him a job.

Her name was Ceridwen and she was an enchantress, not that Gwion knew what that was. She charmed a suit of armour for her giant husband, Tegid Foel, to protect him in battle.

She taught her daughter, Creirfyw, to sing sweeter than a linnet. And now she was gathering toadstools, slime moulds and swamp smells to make a potion to give her son, Morfran, the powers of imagination and inspiration, for with those he would become a sorcerer or superhero.

The potion had to boil in an iron cauldron for a year and a day and she needed a boy to pump the bellows to keep the fire burning, preferably one who'd never had a single thought in his life. Gwion had the ideal qualifications.

So, he sat by the cauldron and kept the fire alight and the potion boiling for a year and a day, until Ceridwen told him to pump the bellows one last time. The fire flamed and frightened Gwion so much that he stood up in front of Morfran and raised his arm to protect his face as three drops of potion spat from the cauldron. They burned his hand, it stung, he licked it and swallowed the three drops.

Gwion had a thought.

He'd never had one before.

Was this imagination and inspiration?

He knew Ceridwen was angry, and it would be best to get out of there quick. Gwion bolted through the door and ran like a hare into the woods.

Gwion was right. Ceridwen was fuming. She howled and chased him as a greyhound, and just as her teeth were about to bite into Gwion's back leg, he dived into the river and swam like a salmon.

Ceridwen shrieked and chased him as an otter, and just as her sharp teeth were about to bite into Gwion's fur, he flew into the air like a songbird.

Ceridwen squawked and chased him as a hawk, and just as her claws were about to scratch Gwion's feathers, he swooped through the window of a barn.

He changed into a grain of wheat and hid in the grain store, thinking Ceridwen would never find him here – no way, absolutely not.

Ceridwen swooped through the window, turned herself into a jet-black hen with a red comb, and swallowed the grain that was Gwion.

It was dark and damp inside Ceridwen's belly and Gwion was growing. Nine months later, he was born again as a baby boy. He knew Ceridwen was still angry, so he sang a *cywydd*, a poem-song, to soothe her with his imagination and inspiration. It didn't work. Ceridwen placed him inside a coracle, covered him with skins and launched him into the sea at the mouth of the Dyfi Estuary. The coracle ebbed and flowed on the tide until it was caught in a seine net by a young fisherman called Elffyn.

Elffyn hoped the coracle contained gold, because with gold he could be the poet he had always dreamed of. So, baby Gwion sang a *cywydd* to explain that one day he'd be worth more than gold.

Elffyn showed the baby to his father, Gwyddno Garanhir, Lord of the now-submerged land of Cantre'r Gwaelod.

'What have you caught, my boy? A nice salmon?'

Elffyn replied, 'Er, I think it's a poet.'

Gwyddno laughed, 'A poet won't fill my belly. Throw it back.'

Baby Gwion sang a *cywydd* to ask them to raise him there on the banks of the Dyfi, where his imagination and inspiration would fill their bellies. And Gwion was right, for he grew to be a great poet, and they named him Taliesin.

Not bad for a boy who never had a single thought.

Red Dragon

Vortigern, King of the Brythons, was a rubbish King. He was trying to build a castle at Dinas Emrys in Snowdonia, but every morning he woke up to find the walls had fallen down. He had a tantrum and told his workers to rebuild the castle, but the walls kept crumbling. His advisers explained that the gods were angry, and to make them happy he must sacrifice a child. So, the people hid their children in the forest to save them from this crazy-mad King.

Only one boy stayed behind. Emrys Wledig had the skills of a sorcerer, a conjurer and a magician. Though he didn't wear round glasses and a black cape. He just stared at people. It was disturbing.

Emrys was brought before Vortigern.

'Excellent, this boy will make a fine sacrifice.'

'No, I won't,' said Emrys, who wasn't afraid of a King.

'You will do as my advisors say.'

'Your advisers are wrong. The gods aren't angry. Do you know the story of Lludd, the wisest of all the Kings of the Brythons?' and he stared at Vortigern.

'Wiser than me?'

'Totally! He had a red dragon.'

Emrys began, 'Long ago, Brython was cursed by a plague of screams and shrieks. Lludd knew the scream was the battle cry of a white dragon and its army of Saxons, and the shriek was his own red dragon fighting the invaders.

'So Lludd hatched a cunning plan. He went to Oxford, where the dragons were fighting, dug a pit, placed a cauldron inside, filled it with mead and covered it in silk. The dragons landed on the silk, fell into the cauldron, drank the mead and fell asleep. Lludd dragged the dozy dragons here to Dinas Emrys and locked them in an underground stone cell.'

Emrys stared at Vortigern, 'You are building your castle on top of the underground stone cell and the dragons have been woken by the noise and are fighting again. If the white dragon wins, Brython will be ruled by the Saxons and you will be killed. But if the red dragon wins, Brython will be saved.'

'And why should I believe a scruffy child rather than my educated advisors?'

'Easy. Dig a hole down to the underground stone cell and help the red dragon chase the white dragon away.'

So Vortigern dug a deep hole and released the dragons. The red dragon chased away the Saxons and Brython was saved, exactly as Emrys predicted. Though the people still thought Vortigern was a clown, so they chased him away too, all the way to the cliffs at Carreg y Llam at Nant Gwrtheyrn, where he jumped into the sea and was never seen again.

The people built a new country and called it Cymru, and a clever illustrator drew a red dragon on the flag of Wales.

And that wise young man, Emrys Wledig? Many stories were told about him, and he became known as Myrddin. Merlin.

And the Welsh? **Yma** *o* **hyd**!

Make a crankie

When you tell the stories in this book, maybe illustrate them with a mini-crankie. All you need are a matchbox, two long matchsticks, a scroll of paper, scissors, marker pens or paints and tape.

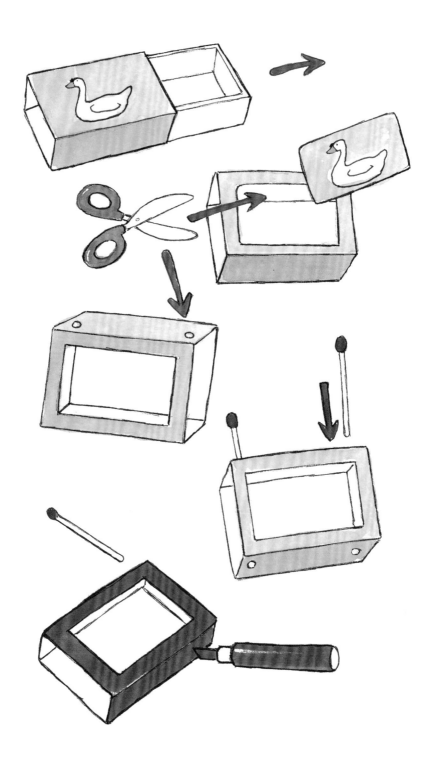

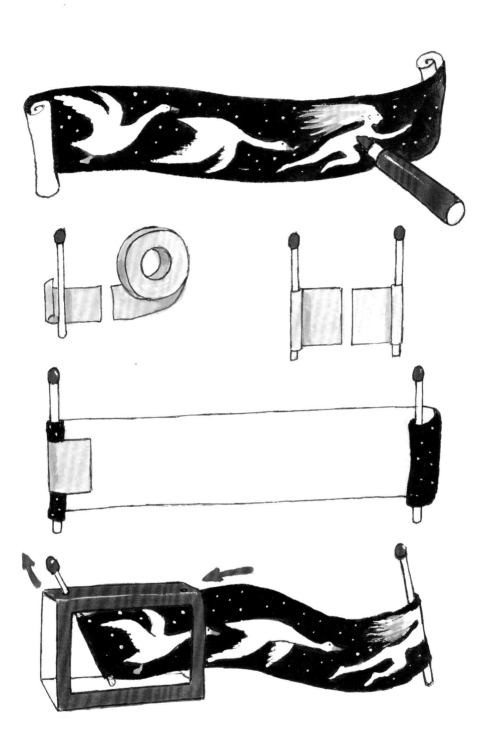

Most of the folk tales in this book have their roots in real places. 'The Land Beneath the Sea' and 'Mermaids' are both from **Cardigan Bay**; 'Swan Girl' and 'Ceffyl Dŵr', **Gower**; 'Red Dragon', **Dinas Emrys**; 'Arthur', **Craig y Ddinas**; 'Afanc', **Conwy**; 'Jemima Fawr', **Fishguard**; 'The Wolfhound', **Beddgelert**; 'The Coal Giant', **Rhymney**; 'Moon Girl', **Snowdon**; 'The Fairy Cow', **Llyn Barfog**; 'The Red Lady', **Trychrug**; 'Shemi the Fibber', **Wdig**; 'The Boy Who Wore a Frock', **Mynydd Bach**; 'The Old Toad', **Cors Fochno**; 'The Red Bandits', **Dinas Mawddwy**; 'The Girl and the Hare', **Pennant Melangell**; 'The Ferny Man', **Garth Mountain**.

Some places are mentioned in the titles: 'The Lady of **Ogmore**'; 'The **Tregaron** Elephant'; 'Cofiwch **Dryweryn**'; and Devil's Bridge is, of course, from '**Devil's Bridge**'.

Some of the stories were told by the same storyteller from the same place, such as Myra Evans from **Cei Newydd**: 'The Little Red Man', 'Mari Lwyd', 'Beti's Love Potions', 'Sgilti the Fiddler', and 'Siani Chickens'.

And Welsh Romany tales like 'The Green Man' and 'The Horse that Pooped Gold' and 'Bag o' Bones' were told wherever travellers pitched their tents. The Welsh Romany storytellers were some of the finest in the land.

Yet all stories migrate. There are tales of people living beneath most lakes in Wales, mermaids frolic all along the coast and y tylwyth teg are up to mischief everywhere. If a storyteller from Aberystwyth tells a tale in another part of Wales and someone likes it enough to tell it themselves, then the story begins its journey.

I've told some of the tales in this book in Appalachia in the USA and in Aotearoa New Zealand, where they are now told by local tellers. I've also been told tales on my travels and have retold them back home in Wales. I ask permission to tell them, of course. That's the way it works.

And finally, a few stories are memories of my childhood, like these from **Pen Llŷn**: 'The House with the Front Door at the Back', 'Donkey's Ears', 'Swan Girl' and 'The Corpse Bride'. And 'Jac-y-do' sort of happened in **Llithfaen**. I learnt most of these from Eddie Kenrick of **Edern**, a friend of my dad's.

Dyna ni. There we are. Now you can tell these tales, and they can root themselves and grow in your own garden.

Society *for*
Storytelling

Since 1993, The Society for Storytelling has championed the ancient art of oral storytelling and its long and honourable history – not just as entertainment, but also in education, health, and inspiring and changing lives. Storytellers, enthusiasts and academics support and are supported by this registered charity to ensure the art is nurtured and developed throughout the UK.

Many activities of the Society are available to all, such as locating storytellers on the Society website, taking part in our annual National Storytelling Week at the start of every February, purchasing our quarterly magazine Storylines, or attending our Annual Gathering – a chance to revel in engaging performances, inspiring workshops, and the company of like-minded people.

You can also become a member of the Society to support the work we do. In return, you receive free access to Storylines, discounted tickets to the Annual Gathering and other storytelling events, the opportunity to join our mentorship scheme for new storytellers, and more. Among our great deals for members is a 30% discount off titles from The History Press.

For more information, including how to join, please visit

www.sfs.org.uk